I0629483

Jerry and Sharon Ahern's

AMERICA UNDEAD

Books by Phil Elmore

Jerry and Sharon Ahern's
America Undead

Coming Soon!
America Undead: America Burning Book 2

Books in The Survivalist Series by Jerry Ahern

#1: Total War	Mid-Wake
#2: The Nightmare Begins	#16: The Arsenal
#3: The Quest	#17: The Ordeal
#4: The Doomsayer	#18: The Struggle
#5: The Web	#19: Final Rain
#6: The Savage Horde	#20: Firestorm
#7: The Prophet	#21: To End All War
#8: The End is Coming	The Legend
#9: Earth Fire	#22: Brutal Conquest
#10: The Awakening	#23: Call To Battle
#11: The Reprisal	#24: Blood Assassins
#12: The Rebellion	#25: War Mountain
#13: Pursuit	#26: Countdown
#14: The Terror	#27: Death Watch
#15: Overlord	

SURVIVE!
Live Well and Live Wisely
Articles by:
Jerry Ahern, Sharon Ahern, Phil Elmore, Jim Cobb, Bob Anderson, Sean Ellis and More

Jerry and Sharon Ahern's

AMERICA UNDEAD

by Phil Elmore

SPEAKING VOLUMES, LLC
NAPLES, FLORIDA
2017

AMERICA UNDEAD

Copyright © 2017 by Jerry Ahern, Sharon Ahern, and Phil Elmore

All rights reserved. No part of this book may be reproduced or transmitted
in any form or by any means without written permission.

ISBN 978-1-62815-767-3

For Jerry

Acknowledgments

Jerry Ahern's books were an inspiration to generations of writers. His influence — and his untimely loss — are felt dearly in these pages.

Foreword

"America Undead" began as the brainchild of Jerry and Sharon Ahern. Jerry was one of the few authors to whom I ever wrote a fan letter. It was sometime during the late 1990s that I received a letter in return from Jerry. It was printed on a dot matrix printer and was extremely gracious. I don't know if he ever knew how much that meant to me.

Over the years, Jerry and I spoke infrequently. When we connected on social media, I suggested offhand that if Jerry ever wanted to work on anything together, I would dearly love to do so. Jerry and Sharon's work — in The Survivalist, The Takers, The Freeman, and The Defender — figured prominently in my influences and inspirations as an author. It was with the lessons of The Survivalist in mind that I approached my work on the Mack Bolan/Stony Man/Executioner series for many years.

When Jerry and Sharon asked me to collaborate on America Undead, it was a dream come true. Sadly, Jerry passed away before the manuscript was complete, but I like to think this book honors the work he and Sharon have done. Hopefully, it also adds to that body of work in a credible and entertaining way. The Aherns have influenced my own writing profoundly; any errors on these pages are mine, but if you like what you read here, that's solely due to Jerry and Sharon Ahern.

Phil Elmore, October 2017

Chapter One

Transylvania, 1462 A.D.

The pain was unbearable.

Altan bin Ramseur's eyes shot open. He was again staring at the grain of the bloody pike that had been rammed through his body. He put his hands on the stake and, as he had tried a hundred times before, struggled to move the wooden stake.

The scream that escaped his throat left flecks of blood on his lips. He was dying.

Again.

The end would come soon. And then he would wake and begin to die once more.

Altan bin Ramseur was not entirely alone in his torment. Impaled with him, arranged in concentric circles that filled the small valley of mud and blood and broken weapons, were hundreds of corpses. Each had been speared, as he was, from anus to chest. The highest of these was the stake of Hamza Pasha, once tribal leader of Actia Nicopolis.

The privileges of rank, thought bin Ramseur.

But for all his status, Hamza Pasha was dead, left to rot on the end of a pike with the men in his commend. Only Altan bin Ramseur lived, to die and live and die again, trapped in an earthly Hell without end.

"I consign you to the misery that is not death, but life." That is what Vlad Tepes had said to him, before his sharpened teeth bit deeply into bin Ramseur's throat, spraying Altan bin Ramseur with a torrent of his own blood...

He shook his head, as if he could hurl the memory from inside his own skull. The movement intensified the agony of the pike through his body, causing his congealing blood to well from his mouth and ooze down his chin.

Allah, he prayed. *Thou who art great. Allah, grant me death. I beg you.*

Egyptian vultures wheeled in lazy pairs above the forest of impaled corpses. The birds were feasting on the dead, heavy as they gorged themselves, in no hurry as they plucked at the eyes, the skin, the flesh of Altan bin Ramseur's fellow soldiers.

The force of 10,000 horsemen led by Hamza Pasha had been sent to put down Vlad Tepes, Prince of Wallachia, for the latter's impudent refusal to pay proper tribute to the Ottoman Empire. Dracula's refusal to pay the *Jizya*, a tax on infidels within his lands, had been the final insult. Vlad Tepes and his father were members of the Order of the Dragon, devoted as it was to the protection of Christendom. Dracula, the son of the Devil, would fall before Turkish swords. So it would be.

Altan bin Ramseur had ridden proudly to what would be his horrible defeat.

Easy victory had been theirs, or so bin Ramseur had believed. But the Turks had been defeated. Many thousands of men had already been impaled when Altan bin Ramseur himself fell before his foes.

But they had not killed him. They had not staked him out to die. They had made Altan bin Ramseur their prisoner.

It was a casual contempt, an insult intended to disgrace him. While their men were to be slaughtered, the Turkish officers were spared and clapped in irons. They were then dragged behind Vlad Tepes' column as the Wallachians marched for Turkish soil in a mad bid to take revenge, claiming they would murder the Sultan himself.

Dracula's desire for vengeance had outstripped his resources. The Wallachians were turned back, driven out of lands nominally held by the Turks long before there was or could be any danger to the Sultan. But still Altan bin Ramseur was dragged by his enemies, forced to trod through the filth of the animals, surviving on whatever scraps were left in the dirt for him to snatch up in his trek.

He had been astonished by the cruelty of Vlad Tepes' men. Even as they retreated, the Wallachians scorched the earth as they passed, torturing, raping, and murdering all they encountered as they fled back to their country. The impudence of it made bin Ramseur's blood boil.

His thirst for recompense had driven him to folly. Every time his eyes opened to behold the bloody wooden pike, every time he felt anew the misery that was living death on the stake, he cursed his foolhardy pride. But he was forced to relive the memories again and again.

Altan bin Ramseur had waited for his moment. Dracula himself had allowed the prisoners to draw even with him as they marched. Vlad Tepes' opulently appointed mount had snorted and pawed the earth as the Wallachian prince brought the animal up short. The guards paused to bow in tribute to their leader, and that had included the slave-master, the man around whose neck was worn the iron key to the prisoners' shackles.

The slave-master wore a sword.

That sword would be in Altan bin Ramseur's hand, or he would die trying to take it.

As the Wallachians bowed to their prince, bin Ramseur, judging the distance short enough, had sprung. He leapt on the man like an animal, clawing at his eyes, striking at his throat. The sword nearly sprang into bin Ramseur's shaking hands as, weakened from lack of food and the abuse he had suffered, the Turk nonetheless rammed the tip of the blade through the slave-master's neck.

Blood sprayed him, hot and thick. He opened his mouth and tasted it, swallowed it, ripping the key on its leather thong from around the slave-master's throat. He was pulling free from his chains when the first of Vlad Tepes' personal guard fell on him, their swords naked in their fists and death in their eyes. Altan bin Ramseur, a Turk Captain, was free and armed in the presence of their Prince. They would die before they would let bin Ramseur pass.

Dracula, son of the Devil, waited astride his horse. He did not speak. He did not move. He did not blink.

Altan bin Ramseur roared his defiance.

Two blades converged on him, wielded by two of the guards. He swatted these away with his stolen sword, coming in under the attack, carving away the first man's arm from beneath. On the second he won a deep cut through the bicep, and on the return of his whirling blade, he slashed them both across the neck. Again he stood in a fountain of blood as Dracula's forces fell away from him.

Vlad Tepes snapped his fingers.

Four more of Dracula's personal guards charged him. He parried, dodged, stepped away, and still they came, chopping and hacking at him. Without thinking he maneuvered to attack the knot of men at the corner, angling to put the guards in one another's way, so that they must fight through each other to reach him. The slave-master's sword, poorly balanced compared to his own well-used scimitar, felt heavy in his hand. The tip of the blade began to drop as his strength flagged.

You disgrace yourself, he had thought to himself then, delirious with the thought he might fight his way free. *You are a Captain in the army of Sultan Mehmed-i sani, el-Fatih, Mehmet II, the Conqueror. You are a soldier, as was your father, and his father before him. You stood on the bloody stones of Constantinople when it fell. You have killed many infidels in the service of Allah and of el-Fatih. You are stronger than this.*

The Turk felt his back straighten. He screamed a curse on the infidels and lunged, spearing the first of Dracula's four guards through the neck. Ripping the blade through the side of the man's throat, he slashed the second man across the face and, as he recoiled, he drove the sword up under the man's arm, through his armpit, deep into his body.

Abandoning the trapped blade, bin Ramseur snatched the nearly identical sword from the dying guard's hand, bringing it up in time to smash the flat of the blade against the cutting edge of the third man's weapon. The fourth drove in low, practically on one knee, and tried to cut through bin Ramseur's guard. The Turk was ready for the maneuver and flicked the tip of the sword into the man's eyes.

He had time to cut the third guard's throat and advance another step—

He stood before the horse of Vlad Tepes, only paces away from killing the prince of Wallachia.

Behind the Turk, the blinded guard wailed, crawling in the dirt on hands and knees. Vlad Tepes' brow furrowed. He dismounted, walked past Altan bin

Ramseur as if the man were not there, and drew the jeweled sword he carried at his side. The Turk stared in disbelief. He could not bring himself to strike.

The Wallachian forces closed in, forming a circle around bin Ramseur and Dracula.

"I was raised among you," said Dracula in Turkish. "I know you value courage as highly as do I. And I know that even among Turks, the failure of a man to protect his master is a grievous one."

Altan bin Ramseur said nothing. Vlad Tepes shrugged, very faintly, and drove his sword through the chest of the blind man. The guard made a choking sound, a bleat of pain and surprise, before collapsing on the ground. A pool of blood began to grow about him.

"You are the son of the Devil," said bin Ramseur to his enemy.

"I am the son of Vlad the Second," said Dracula, patiently, even with condescension, as if he were instructing a stubborn pupil. "Like my father, I am of the Order of the Dragon. We will protect Christendom from those such as you. We will wage war on the Ottoman Turks. There is nothing you can do to stand before us."

"I stand before you," said the Turk. "I, Altan bin Ramseur, shall be the sword of the Sultan. You will fall before me, Dracula. Or do you fear me?"

Dracula laughed. The sound was liquid, deep and full of mirth. "You wish to face me, Turk? You wish the honor of dying at the hand of Vlad Tepes? So it shall be. No man shall touch him!" He spoke now to his troops. "No man shall harm Altan bin Ramseur, even if I fall."

Dracula charged as he spoke the last few words.

He was a cunning foe. Few men could talk and fight. The son of the Devil knew well that a man whose mind was fixed on speech would be ill-prepared for a sudden advance. The Turk barely parried the blade before mounting an attack of his own, slashing and hacking, hammering away as Dracula blocked the blows that rained upon his sword.

"They say that you eat flesh," bin Ramseur said, breathing heavily as he fought. "They say that you drink blood. Well, I have drunk much blood this day, and I shall taste... *yours*!"

As he said it, the Turk described an arc with his blade that cut deeply down and across Dracula's neck. The blade of bin Ramseur's sword caught in the edge of the leather breastplate Dracula wore. He dragged it free as Dracula fell, first to one knee, then the other. The breastplate, its ties severed, fell free, exposing Dracula's chest.

Bin Ramseur knew this would be his last deed. Despite Vlad Tepes' orders, the Wallachians would close and slaughter him when they realized he had killed their prince. He did not care.

He would gladly pay the cost of his life for the honor of killing this man.

The Turk took a single step forward. He brought his sword back, ready to chop the head from Dracula's neck.

Let them put my body on a pike, he thought. *Their master will go to Hell sundered, without his head, there to suffer for eternity.*

The flesh of Dracula's wounded neck began to knit before his eyes.

Altan bin Ramseur's mouth opened. Whatever words he may have spoken died in his throat. The injury he had dealt Dracula was vanishing while he watched. What sorcery was this?

Dracula smiled. He moved as if to rise, to regain his feet. His jeweled sword started to come up—

"God is great!" screamed Altan bin Ramseur. He ran Dracula through with his sword.

Vlad Tepes fell to the ground, dead, as blood gushed from the wound in his chest.

The Turk froze. There was not a word from the assembled Wallachians. They stood as if rooted to the ground, their hands on their weapons, their eyes on their dead prince. Any moment now and the spell would be broken. They would bellow their outrage and descend on him. They would rip him limb from limb.

He was ready. He was ready to die. Surely he would go to Paradise. Surely he had earned his way.

A murmur rose from the watching soldiers.

Vlad Tepes stood.

The Prince of Wallachia might have been sleeping, save for the blood staining his fine robes. He advanced on Altan bin Ramseur and his knuckles were white on his sword. His face was a mask of rage.

"Sorcery!" bin Ramseur gasped. He could not believe his eyes.

"You!" Dracula screamed. He dropped his sword and swatted away the blade in Altan bin Ramseur's hand. The shock of the blow astonished the Turk. Dracula had the strength of many men, easily. The bones in bin Ramseur's hand felt as if they had shattered.

Now Dracula's hands were around his throat.

Feeling his eyes bulge, feeling his world gray and blackening and close around him, Altan bin Ramseur went to his knees in the bloody dirt while Dracula choked him. He did not understand. He had won. He had killed the son of the Devil.

He was to die at the hands of a man who was himself already dead.

As his senses threatened to leave him, the Turk heard Dracula whispering into his ear. It was then that he saw the man's teeth. They were filed, yes, sharpened to needle points... but Dracula also had fangs. These were long, sharp, and unlike any teeth that filled a mortal man's jaw.

He truly is the son of the Devil, thought the Turk.

"You dare strike me down in the presence of my men?" Dracula asked him. His hands were like iron on bin Ramseur's neck. The Turk struggled, clawing and scratching and pulling at the fingers around his throat, but the red marks healed almost instantly. "I am not going to kill you, Turk," hissed Vlad Tepes. "I am going to make you suffer. Your torment shall be unlike any faced by man, alive or dead. For I shall do both to you. I consign you to the misery that is not death, but life."

The Son of the Devil had sunk his fangs deep in bin Ramseur's throat, then, ripping away a chunk of flesh that left a ragged, bloody hole in his victim's neck. As everything turned black, Altan bin Ramseur knew he would awake screaming, for he had relived these memories a hundred times. Each time, he awoke to the field of impaled bodies. Each time, he remembered the curse placed on him by the son of the Devil.

He was damned to live and die forever.

The pain was unbearable.

His eyes snapped open once more. He blinked. The pike had moved. As it moved, the pain had grown worse.

It happened again. Then it happened once more. Feverish in his torture, bin Ramseur realized only then that he was being chopped down. A woman and two young girls, neither yet of child-bearing age, were hacking at the pike with axes. One of the girls, seeing bin Ramseur stir, looked up and pointed. She spoke to the woman, presumably her mother, and the other young girl nodded.

They knew. They had been watching. They had seen him die and come once more to life.

With a splintering and cracking, tearing at Altan bin Ramseur's body from within, the pike collapsed. He felt his bones crack, his ribs give away, as the ground rushed up to strike him. Through his darkening vision he saw the woman cross herself. She wore a wooden pendant, this too in the shape of a cross, on a leather thong about her neck.

Christians. They were Christians.

They were saving him.

Death claimed him once more. When he awoke again, it was to the astonishing sensation that there was no pain. They had pulled him free of the pike. He was bloody, he was weak, but he was no longer a prisoner. As he stared up at the woman and her daughters, they spoke over him with their eyes closed.

They are praying for me, he thought. *I am saved.*

He tried to speak, but his throat, though healed, was dry. His words were a croak. The woman's eyes opened and she looked down at him. She was beautiful. She smiled and said something he could not understand.

Altan bin Ramseur grabbed her by the hair and bit deeply into her neck, tearing out her throat.

Chapter Two

Twenty Years Ago

The odors of rain and human blood brushed her lips. Elizabeth Hawkins touched the door panel and raised the Cadillac's window against the night air. Except for the windshield wipers, her eyes detected no movement. For her, there were no shadows, even at this late hour.

Her night vision was exceptionally keen, even for a vampire.

"Shares in UconWep, the nation's leading small arms manufacturer, rose again despite the dip in industry averages and a decline in tech sector—" She frowned and stabbed the faceplate of the radio with her index finger. The unit scanned available frequencies and settled on two more news stations before alighting on classical music. She withdrew her hand. That would do.

The waiting was beginning to irritate her. Brasov should have been here half an hour ago. From the deep, custom-tailored pockets of her leather overcoat, she removed her Glock 26 pistols, each bearing the logo of a company long nationalized and dissolved. Beneath the stylized "G" on the pistols' slides was the UconWep star. *The world's leading manufacturer of replica firearms*. The jingle came to her, unbidden, the result of countless television, radio, and webstream commercials.

"No wonder their stock always goes up," she said to no one. Never mind the fact that the stock market, these days, was itself a sham, a puppet show for the masses who still believed some shred of capitalist motivation drove the economy.

She press-checked each Glock replica before returning them to their places in her coat. She had checked them once already, of course. To be reduced to nervous tics brought color to her cheeks. Damn Woodrow Brasov, anyway.

She exhaled, reigning in her temper.

He was a busy man, after all. The hero of Operation Just Vengeance, the symbol of the Fifth Islamic War, could hardly be expected to adhere strictly to schedules. At least not to *other* people's schedules.

Beneath her, the oily waters of the Potomac were black beneath the falling mist. From this end of the bridge, she could just make out the opposite side. She blinked as high-intensity blue-white headlights signaled the approach of Brasov's Town Car.

"It's about damned time," she said quietly. She checked her phone, strapped beneath her wrist, and made sure there were no message telltales. None of her people had broken wireless silence. They were disciplined and they were loyal.

A tall man — he was indeed the right height for Brasov, and wore Brasov's trademark belted raincoat and matching black fedora — stepped from the vehicle, snapping his collar up around his neck. Through the mist, as she began to cross the bridge, Hawkins could see the blood-red tie at his throat. It was the only color the man wore.

He moved briskly toward her and she went to meet him. At the midpoint of the bridge she offered him a jaunty wave. "Vlad!" she called, smiling. "I have seen today's polls. Is it premature to call you 'Mister President?'"

Brasov said something unintelligible. The smell of humanity began to grow stronger. Elizabeth could not place it; wet weather wreaked hell with her heightened sense of smell. As she came to within a few paces of Brasov, however, she sensed the danger: There were other vampires, close by. Her own people were well back. These could be nothing but enemies.

She heard the *snick* of a bolt being run back.

"Shit! Vlad! It's a setup!" She tackled Brasov before he could react.

From boats in the water below, Kalashnikov-pattern rifles opened up, spraying the bridge with automatic fire. Brasov struggled beneath her as she lay across his chest. She grunted as a round ripped through her calf, ruining her high leather boot, and another tore at the pavement inches from her face. The gunfire could not kill her, except in the most unlikely of circumstances, but it could slow her down long enough for her enemies to burn or decapitate her. She would not allow that.

She tried to bring her left wrist to her face to call for help, summon her backup. Brasov snatched her wrist.

Except that it wasn't Brasov. This man was not even a vampire. The stink of his human blood was suddenly overpowering; her own adrenaline had briefly masked the scent. The imposter, obviously chosen for his height and resemblance to the presidential candidate, was drawing a .45 automatic from within his raincoat.

She had been betrayed.

Elizabeth snarled and swatted the 1911 from the man's hand, snapping his wrist. His howl of pain was cut short as she ripped out his throat, drinking deeply of the torrent this released. Drawing her pistols from the pockets of her coat, she sprang forward, running and dodging with inhuman speed. There was no cover on the bridge. The Town Car was closer and the only cover to be had. She ran for it.

Helicopters whispered into position above the bridge, held aloft by cushions of forced air from their muffled turboprops. From the open bays of these, more gunmen —human or vampire, she could not tell — opened fire, raking the bridge and staggering her as more holes were punched through her body. Vampires leapt the sides of the bridge, swarming from beneath, where perhaps they had concealed themselves by clinging to the girders below. She smelled them before she saw them. They carried machetes and automatic weapons.

They were here to kill her.

Oh, Vlad, she thought. *You clever, clever bastard.* It was a setup... but not to assassinate Brasov. He had known she would come when called; she had made no secret of her desire to ally more directly with his forces, especially with the Cousinry hunting her.

Apparently the answer was no.

The tactics employed by Brasov's kill team would be simple enough. It had taken only days since the first vampires outed themselves for their human cousins to work out what humans called *the rules*. Vampires breathed — it would be hard for them to speak, otherwise, for how did one operate vocal cords without breath — but to kill one by choking, strangling, or smothering would take *weeks* of constant deprivation. Sunlight burned them, and badly, but not badly enough to kill except in extreme cases. Certainly they did not burst into flame from the touch of an errant sunray. A stake through the heart, of iron or wood, was debilitating but not immediately fatal.

No, to kill a vampire required the liberal application of fire... or the separation of the head from the body. Shoot a vampire and he would quickly heal... but shoot him over and over again, with an automatic weapon, and you could buy time to burn him or cut off his head. Human and vampire alike had taken to carrying firearms and blades, flamethrowers and even Molotov cocktails, when facing vampires, whose greater speed and strength made them formidable enemies.

Brasov's clever trap was meant to remove Elizabeth Hawkins from the chessboard that was ever in Vlad's mind. Very well. At least she knew where she stood.

Or crouched.

Taking shelter behind the engine block of the Town Car, which was armored as Vlad's would have been, she let the sleek black automobile absorb the worst of the automatic gunfire trained her way. Vlad's kill team was advancing on her, walking across the bridge formed in ranks, leaving not an inch for her to squeeze through.

She tried the passenger-side door. It was locked. Neither the bullets from her Glocks nor the vampire strength in her arms would pull it free.

Vlad had always been good with details. It was what she had always loved about him. Evil, smart, completely ruthless. He was still the fifteenth century warrior he had always been. The thrill of his touch, the danger of his presence, had nearly overpowered her when they had first met, late in the 20th century.

She would have to talk to him about his trap when next she saw him. Perhaps she would wrap his precious United Nations Medal of Courage around his throat...

The kill team was almost close enough. She brought her wrist to her lips. Her breath activated her phone.

"*Fiat lux*," she whispered.

White phosphorous flares, fired from launchers held by her own people, burned white and brilliant against the nighttime cloud cover. Gunfire from the opposite end of the bridge began to pick out targets among the kill team. The screams, and the fact that three men fell dead from headshots, told her Vlad's people had human mercenaries mixed among them. That would be Caspian and his thermal scope, picking out the heat signatures of the warm-blooded living from among the... less so.

The vampires among Vlad's shooters continued to press her position, undaunted. She was tired of playing the victim. A touch of her finger brought up the remote control application on her phone.

"Engine start," she said quietly.

Brilliant plasma headlights arced across the bridge. Her Cadillac smart-car's oversized engine growled against its sound baffles. She drew her finger across the face of her wrist phone and the car surged forward, its tires slipping, squcaling, and finally catching on the wet pavement.

The vampires were quick, but some were faster than others. The Cadillac crushed three of them as it barreled through their ranks. Bones cracked. At least one head was separated from its neck. That enemy would not trouble her again.

With her mini-Glocks filling her fists, she squeezed the triggers again and again, charging the enemy, closing the remaining distance. Her bullets found their mark and staggered one, then another, then a third foe. Then the pistols were empty. There was no time to reload; there was no time to pocket them. She let them fall from her hands.

The practical wakizashi, a modern, single-edged blade with a swept cutting profile, was firm in her grip, its rubber handle giving her ample traction. She brought the blade up and out from beneath her coat. The small oval guard of the wakizashi was barely enough to protect her hand, but this was a weapon designed for speed at close quarters, patterned after the "indoor" blade of Japan's samurai warriors. She brought the razor-sharp edge up through the chest of the nearest vampire, laying him open from belly to neck.

The smell of his blood hit her.

Flesher, she thought. A barbarian who still regularly fed on humans. Of course Vlad, throwback that he was, would employ killers of this type. It was rumored that Brasov himself still fed on humankind, violating the most important tenet of their kin, the source and the point of contention for the uneasy truce that existed between mortal men and the nearly immortal undead. Not a week went by that some report of a vampire lynching — something of a misnomer, as fire or decapitation were invariably used — did not receive mention in the news. It was usually followed by a vampire reprisal, in which the drained corpses of humans were left somewhere prominent and suitably ghastly. This would in turn fuel another lynching, and so on.

Stupid, she thought. *Stupid and short-sighted*. Not that the Cousinry's ranks were any better. They paid lip-service to non-aggression with humans, but their methods were inconsistent and, to her mind, ineffective.

She brought her blade quickly across the flesher's throat, then again, then hacked a third time, finally severing his head from his body. The pair behind the vampire held broad-bladed axes. Their bodies were riddled with bullet holes, these rapidly healing.

It was their proximity to Elizabeth that had saved them. Her people were spraying the bridge in fusillade after fusillade, emptying their submachineguns and assault rifles to keep Brasov's team pinned. They could fire no closer to Elizabeth, however, without risking hitting her, which might slow her enough for her foes to take her down. Likewise, the angle of the bridge struts from where she now stood would prevent Caspian from getting a clear shot with his heavy .50-caliber rifle.

That's what the car was for.

The Cadillac, propelled by her remote control, slammed into the two vampires from behind, snapping their spines. They were crushed beneath its heavy front tires. She stroked her phone again and the smart-car reversed itself, heeling about, then surged ahead once more crushing the two killers under its wheels. She moved with the car, letting it shield her. It was lightly armored against small arms fire, more than sufficient for this purpose.

Brasov's reserve forces were beginning to close from the end of the bridge where the Town Car sat. One of their bullets clipped her in the shoulder. She ran, tapping her phone furiously as she did so, dodging and ducking as the big car rolled around to meet her. It executed a rapid reverse turn and the rear door snapped open. She hurled herself inside, throwing her bloody, bared sword to the carpeted floor.

"Home, James," she said.

The Cadillac's tires squealed as it labored to put them back at its starting point, which for this moment was the opposite end of the bridge. Bullets *spanged* from the armored windshield and windows.

"I'm clear," she said into her phone. She paused, considering. The intensity of her response would determine just how completely she burned her connection to Brasov.

"Fire the village," she said at last.

Sorry Vlad, she thought. *We'll always have Paris.*

Well. It wasn't as romantic as it might have been — the time she and Vlad, working to incite a Muslim mob, had worked to burn *down* Paris. But he had taken her atop the hood of a burning car nonetheless, scant feet from flames that could have consumed them both, and she had never known anything like it before or since.

Vlad loved an angry mob. Every man had hobbies.

From their positions on either side of the bridge, her own people, the private army maintained by Elizabeth Hawkins, loyal to her and to the money she paid them, proved their loyalty to her cult of personality. They waded into Brasov's men, wielding flamethrowers and swords and automatic weapons of their own, ripping the ranks of Vlad's soldiers to shreds. She watched from the relative safety of the Cadillac as the battle raged. She was losing vampires, but Vlad's humans had been killed to the last man, his ranks of undead first decimated, then annihilated. Caspian maintained a steady stream of sniper fire from the parapet at the strut on her end of the bridge. She had never found the sound of his rifle more comforting.

Then it was over.

"They are withdrawing," said Caspian's voice through her phone. His Spanish accent was thick with stress. "Shall I call in the Cobra to mop up? Or shall I let them go?"

"No," said Elizabeth. "Kill every last one. Leave no survivors."

"As you wish."

Twenty minutes more was all it took. The last shots were echoing across the river when she left the Cadillac, retracing her steps. The bridge was thick with blood. Caspian, frowning , joined her as she walked, his rifle slung across his back. He held a replica Glock 18 machine pistol in his fists, which were covered in supple black gloves. His silk shirt was open at the throat. She felt a surge of desire as he approached, his long, curly hair flying about his shoulders like a dark lion's mane.

"You should stay in the car."

"I want my pistols," she said. It did not take her long to find them. Caspian frowned as she returned them to the pockets of her leather coat.

"We could get you more."

"These are mine," she reminded him. "What is our status?"

Caspian considered the gold Rolex on his wrist. "We are running out of credit with the District of Columbia police," he said. "It would be wise to leave now and avoid tempting them further."

"Vlad's ambushers?"

"Dead to a man," said Caspian. "And a woman. We could have taken prisoners."

"They would have told you nothing," she said, shaking her head. Her auburn hair brushed her high cheekbones. She saw him notice it.

"They were Brasov's people, yes," said Caspian. "But they are not invincible. He cannot hold them *all* in fear so complete that we could not break one."

"We both know what this was about, Caspian. Vlad does not want me — us — in his club."

"He wishes to control you," said Caspian. "You are not controllable."

"And you of all people would know that best," she said.

"And Brasov? How well does he know you?"

"Caspian," she laughed, gesturing for him to follow as she returned to her Cadillac. "I think you are jealous."

"I do not trust Brasov."

"I *never* did," she said. "Now take me home to bed."

"As you wish." This time, he smiled.

She smiled back. The expression did not touch her eyes. She could not afford to let him see how badly this betrayal had burned her; could not allow him to understand where and how she could be hurt.

It was just as well. She would be thinking of Vlad the entire time... but Caspian did not need to know that, either.

Chapter Three

Tomorrow — The Here And Now, Georgia, United States

The face that stared back from the rearview mirror was ashen, the eyes red-rimmed. His cheeks were drawn. He had not shaved in several days; the graying stubble on his cheeks matched the close-cropped, steel-gray hair on his head. While his strong jaw and chiseled features would probably still be considered handsome to most women — despite his prematurely silver hair, he looked and felt, most days, as if he were still in his thirties — he was not himself, and he knew it. The strain of the last few weeks had been considerable.

Vincent Harden pulled the antique Shelby Cobra through the circular drive of the sheltered estate, grateful for the heavily laden, strategically placed trees that obscured the small mansion from the main road well beyond. He did not wish to be seen coming here. He felt like a ghoul, like a vulture, coming to await his mentor's end.

Arturo, Thomas Simpson's head of security, answered the front door before Harden could raise the brass knocker. He nodded, gesturing for Harden to enter. The stone-faced Sikh wore a long, wickedly curved Jordanian combat knife strapped to his thigh. Over his shoulders he wore a leather holster bearing a 1911-pattern .45 and a pair of extra magazines.

Behind the Sikh, several of Thomas Simpson's staff were visible in the kitchen. The tension was thick. They were waiting, as Harden had been. They were waiting for Thomas Simpson to die.

"He's in his room?" Harden asked. Arturo shook his head. "The study?"

Arturo nodded. Harden made his way to the rear of the first floor and into the extensive library. Here, bookshelves lined the walls, neatly arrayed from floor to ceiling. Harden went to a very specific volume of Revolutionary War history and tugged the spine. This released a catch that allowed him to swing the entire bookshelf out on oiled hinges. Thomas Simpson's hidden study lay within.

"Vincent. You came after all."

Harden paused, forcing himself not to react. It had been a week since he had last seen his dear friend. Thomas had visibly declined. His cheeks were hollow, his skin translucent. He lay on the divan that someone, probably Arturo, had pulled to the front of his ancient oak desk. A tablet computer sat before him, angled so its camera could pick him up. When he reached for it, his hand shook. His veins were distended and looked black beneath his skin.

"I don't agree with this," said Harden. "This... this suicide. Thomas, there's so much more you could do."

Thomas coughed. His painfully thin shoulders heaved up and down. Harden rushed to the side of the divan, thinking Simpson was having convulsions. But that wasn't it at all.

Thomas Simpson was laughing.

"Do more?" the man asked. "Do *more*? Haven't I done *enough*, Vincent?" The recrimination, the bitterness in his voice, had crept slowly into Simpson's words, growing quickly in the last few years. It had come to define the man. Hearing it now, Harden almost smashed his hand down on the desk, almost grabbed his old friend by the shoulders to shake him. The thought of how fragile Thomas had become stopped the younger man.

"You have to stop blaming yourself."

"I will," said Thomas. "Soon enough." He shook his head and gestured for Harden to come closer. "I know you don't like it. I know you think I'm quitting, Vincent. But... I'm so tired. So very tired. I need you to let me go, boy. I need you to give me your blessing."

At the look in Simpson's eyes, Harden cracked. He knelt next to the divan and took Thomas' skeletal hand in his own palms. "Of course. Of course I do. I'm sorry. I just don't know how the Cousinry will manage without you. How I'll manage."

"I would not have chosen you to succeed me if I thought you lacked the strength," said Thomas. "Vincent, my greatest regret was once that I did not have children before I was turned. Then I met you. You are what every vampire could be, Vincent. Free of the stain of human blood. Morally pure. Courageous.

You are the son that was never born to me. I have never told you often enough how proud I am of you."

It was a moment before Harden could bring himself to answer that. "Thank you," he finally said. He could feel his voice threatening to crack.

"Did Arturo make you check your weapons?"

"No," said Harden. "He hasn't for years."

"He hasn't spoken for *centuries*," said Thomas, "but that doesn't mean he won't. Never you mind that. There's something I want you to have. But there's something else we have to do first."

Harden imagined he could hear Thomas' voice weakening with every word. He knew what was coming. He also knew it would take the last of the strength Simpson had left. The elder vampire had been denying himself blood for weeks. He had not taken food or water, either, for to eat or drink while refusing blood would only have prolonged the process. Except for a violent end by blade or fire, this was the only way for a vampire to end his life, as his body slowly consumed itself from within.

"In the center drawer of my desk," wheezed Thomas, "you will find several legal envelopes. These contain everything you'll need, duly witnessed and executed. There are account numbers, a power of attorney, and several other very important details. Instructions. You'll know which are the most sensitive. Memorize them and burn them."

"Of course. Thomas... You're sure about this? About the broadcast?"

"I have hidden long enough," said Simpson. "I have written my will. Now I want to record my last testament. I want you to upload it to the global network. I want the video to go viral. I want it to spread far and wide."

"You don't know that it will," Harden said.

"The truth has a way of doing just that."

"All right." Harden made sure the tablet was running and the recording software was ready. He tapped the device. "When you're ready."

Simpson gathered himself, pushing to a seated position on the divan, his back leaning against the wall of the study for support. When he spoke again, his voice held a shadow of its former strength.

"My name is Thomas Simpson," said the elder vampire. "You have heard my name, although you have not seen my face. In the year of our Lord 1066, at the Battle of Hastings, I was almost four months past my twentieth birthday. On that day I was turned. I became a vampire.

"I, like all of my kind, was made, not born. For centuries, vampires hid themselves from society at large. We were and are governed by the Cousinry, the largest and most secretive fraternal organization the world has known. Working together, we prevented war between humans and vampires, did our best to suppress predation on humans by our kind. Above all, we worked to prevent discovery, for then even the rumors of vampires living among you were enough to spread terror and violence.

"I remember as if it were yesterday the moment that a splinter group of malcontents within the Cousinry, led by the turncoat Elizabeth Hawkins, revealed themselves to you. Early in the 21st century this rogue element sought to trade on the most coveted prize a vampire can offer a human: the promise of near-immortality.

"Hawkins sought power. She wished to command the Cousinry and, after a brief stint as one of my lieutenants, she decided she could run the organization better than I. Her plan was clever and daring, if a bit naive. She hoped to out us and, in so doing, supplant me as the titular head of the vampire community.

"She and her coven of traitors became the center of media frenzy. The public, politicians, celebrities... everyone clamored to be turned, to become immortal. Shrewd, beautiful, and utterly amoral, Hawkins knew how to play to their desires. She organized a series of media sideshows. Her vampires performed foolish feats of speed and strength, proved they could cast reflections and cast water... even endured stakes through the heart to demonstrate the healing powers we possess. It was vulgar. It was disgusting. And it was only the beginning."

Thoughts of Elizabeth Hawkins threatened to turn Harden blind with fury. He focused on his breathing, staring at a spot on the ceiling of the study, trying to calm himself. Thomas either did not notice or had the presence of mind to pretend he did not. Hawkins was a sore subject for them both.

"Hawkins revealed the existence of the Cousinry. She spoke of the great wealth we have amassed, controlled, and managed through the years. She revealed my name as leader of the Cousinry and denounced me as a manipulator. I was, in her words, a tyrant, ruling vampires with an iron fist, refusing humanity the gift she now wished to offer.

"In her arrogance, Hawkins underestimated what we within the Cousinry have known for so long. Fear of us, fear of vampires, overrides even the strongest desire for life in some. When vigilantes struck one of her absurd media events, Hawkins alone escaped with her head. The rest of her vampires were wiped out. She was forced to go into hiding, rebuilding her cult of personality as she fought to stay alive, even as we hunted her for her heinous crimes. But the damage was done. The government now knew of us. Of me. And they made me an offer.

"By that time the Social Democrats had already seized the Presidency and both houses of Congress. The Renewed Deal was well underway. The changes President for Life Woodrow Brasov would enact, by executive order, had forever altered the Constitution of the United States. His rule was without question, his critics summarily imprisoned by the Social Adjustors of his Internal Revenue Squads. I am old enough to remember when the SA stood for something else... but I am an old man.

"Brasov and his army of unelected bureaucrats, his Council of Directors, explained to me that immortality was far too precious a benefit to society not to be governed, not to be controlled. Should the Cousinry wish to turn any more humans into vampires, we would require licenses to do so. And of course I would be presented with a list of men and women. People of power. People of influence. I was instructed to turn them.

"Refuse this request I could... but sooner or later, Hawkins or another like her would come out of hiding. My refusal, I told myself, would only delay the inevitable, now that the Cousinry's secret was revealed.

"Worse, I convinced myself, was the penalty for disobeying Brasov. The Social Democrats own our major news and entertainment media. They have for years. Should I anger Brasov, his people would see to it that the Cousinry was blamed for every major atrocity throughout the last five hundred years of human history. Vampire connections to the Nazis, to the Crusades, to real and imagined illuminati behind every world conflict and economic collapse... some of it true, some of it false, and all of it damning. The Cousinry would become the most hated organization in history, and I would be the Goldstein at its head. For the sake of my people, for the good of the Cousinry, I obeyed."

Thomas' voice was cracking. Harden would have offered him water, even blood, but the room had been swept clean of anything that might prolong the older man's unlife, undoubtedly at Simpson's own order.

"I... tried to explain to Brasov's minions that a newly turned vampire is wild for human blood. To prevent the slaughter of the innocent, he must be contained by others of his own kind until the initial fever of changing passes. Thereafter, like so many of us, he can feed calmly, rationally, from animals. I had not consumed human blood for most of my long life... but I turned those on Brasov's list as they were presented to me.

"Too late I discovered that Brasov had no intention of reining in his new vampires. The Attorney General's newly formed Natural Selective Service, in cooperation with the SA, were combing the streets and alleyways of every major city, sweeping up undesirables, the homeless, illegal immigrants... anyone who would not be missed. You have heard these disappearances blamed on the Cousinry by Brasov's agents. You have believed vampires were responsible. What you have not known is that Brasov and his abominations, not the Cousinry, are behind it.

"When I learned what was going on, I could stand it no more. I resolved to fight. But Brasov no longer needed me. Hawkins had resurfaced, and to her banner flocked every renegade and malcontent within the Cousinry. Together they orchestrated the Day of the Rope, as the public calls it — attacks by Brasov's vampire shock troops on his own newly formed Sharia enclaves throughout the Northeast. These attacks, and the atrocities they spawned, were blamed on the Cousinry. This solidified the enmity between the Cousinry and America's militant Islamist population to this day, and has been used by the media to vilify us as racists, terrorists, and worse to a gullible public.

"Driven even deeper into hiding, I continued to fight Brasov's totalitarian regime. I continued to fight Hawkins and her traitors. I continued to fight the rising tide of Muslim militarization threatening to destroy this nation from within, even as Brasov and the Social Democrats chipped away at its legal and cultural foundations. Now I sit before you, still in hiding, the most wanted fugitive in the world. And I am going to have the last laugh. Because by the time you see this, I will be dead, well beyond the reach of Brasov and his ilk.

"Before I die, however, I wish to say one more thing. The Cousinry is not the enemy of society. Woodrow Brasov is. He must be stopped. His plan is to rule completely, unquestioned and unquestionable, over a divided, dispirited world. But you can fight him.

"Take up arms. Stand your ground. Refuse to comply. Brasov is a vampire, yes. Worse, he is a monster. But he is not invulnerable. He is not invincible. Fight him. Fight his forces. Die on your feet. Or live forever on your knees under the yoke... of his... oppression..."

Harden touched the tablet computer, switching off the video recorder and removing its memory card. He placed the card in his pocket.

Thomas had struggled to get out those last words. Now he slumped on the divan, his eyes closing, his lips peeling back from his teeth. The elongated canines were visible as Harden went to his side, kneeling next to Thomas and cradling the elder vampire's shoulders to support his head.

"How... was it?" Thomas whispered.

"You revealed much," said Harden. "You're certain?"

"Yes."

"Is it... time?"

"Yes. Vincent... my son... you must choose. You can... hide... and support the Resistance from afar... live a long life... be safe. Or you can... fight."

"Stand and fight," said Harden, "or live on my knees. That's no choice at all. I love this country, Thomas. I hate what Brasov and the Social Democrats have done. I'll fight."

"I... knew... you would..." Simpson coughed. The movement shook his whole body. Harden held him close, feeling how weak and insubstantial his second father, his mentor, had become. "In the fire safe under my desk. I have left you my journal. And more instructions. And something... very special. You will know."

24

"All right."

"Brasov might kill you, Vincent. He is a powerful... enemy."

"Brasov can kiss my ass."

Simpson smiled. He returned Harden's embrace. There was movement in the library outside the study. A floorboard creaked. That would be Arturo, wondering if he was needed.

Thomas tried to say something but couldn't manage the words. "Don't try to talk anymore," said Harden. "Please."

"Adam," hissed Simpson, finally. "Adam is the key. He must be protected."

"Yes," Harden said quickly. "I'll do whatever you say. Just please try to stay still."

"Arturo," whispered Simpson. "Arturo."

"I'll explain what happened," said Harden. "He owes you a life-debt, I know. I'll release him from your service."

Simpson shook his head. He gestured with one gnarled hand. "Arturo..." The last word rattled in the older man's lungs. He stared at nothing.

Thomas Simpson was dead.

Harden's head snapped up. The concealed door from the library was ripped open on its hinges. Standing in the doorway, holding a machete and a Mac-11, was the Sikh. He raised the submachinegun.

"Wait," said Harden.

Arturo fired.

Chapter Four

It was the smoke, black and oily, that caught her attention. The dark plume scarring the early-evening sky was the same color as the fumes escaping from her hood. Taggart Jones urged the abused pickup truck forward, watching the RPMs, listening to the ethanol engine scream in protest. Metal grated on metal. She smelled burning oil.

She was not far from Thomas Simpson's estate and the smoke worried her. She had never known the sweet old vampire to burn his trash. She had to assume something was wrong.

"It's the very fact that vampires can't reproduce that *makes* them promiscuous," blared the voice from the truck's radio, some state-controlled propaganda talk broadcast from Chattanooga. "It's a question of nature."

"Just because they're immune to all sexually transmitted diseases doesn't mean they can't pass them on," countered the host. Taggart recognized his voice but could never remember his name. "And what possible reason could a human being have to be attracted to a vampire? Sure, their blood circulates, but they're cold to the touch! It must feel exactly like making love to a corpse. That makes vampire lovers necro—"

She stabbed the button on the dash with her thumb. Enough noise. It wasn't distracting her from the bullet holes in her engine or the body of her truck. This vehicle had pretty much had it, which meant she was out half her transportation.

She had sent her partner, Les Scully, back from the monthly Chattanooga run in the larger truck, breaking off to take a more circuitous route back through Georgia to avoid the roaming patrols of Fedvamps on the border. Besides, if any of the Mutaween were still on their tails, Les, as a man, would fare better talking his way out of one of their improvised roadblocks. The Muslim religious police — technically, the Basij, but commonly referred to as the Mutaween — hated women. They routinely raped those they found alone. What else were chattel good for, after all? It was nothing to them.

Then, too, there was the fact that Taggart was known in the Chattanooga area, her nominal territory as a resistance sympathizer, running crates of ancient Kalashnikovs to the rebel holdouts when she wasn't smuggling liquor into the Sharia enclaves. Every one of the Muslim zones was dry. These local dictates were enforced by the Basij in defiance of Federal regulations saying otherwise. One of Taggart's best customers was Aashif Aziz, personal assistant to the Caliph of Chattanooga. His tastes ran mostly to Gentleman Jack Daniels. She'd been making her way back to the highway, congratulating herself on pocketing a small pile of the Caliph's silver, when the Mutaween had sprung their ambush.

She cursed herself for not anticipating it. She'd become far too regular in her runs to Chattanooga. The Basij had figured out her schedule and simply staked out the major routes in order to intercept her.

She'd taken at least five of them in the gun battle that resulted. Her Thompson submachinegun had served her well. It lay on the seat of the truck next to her, its drum magazine nearly spent. She had a couple of sticks for it loaded yet. She had been lucky to get away with just a ventilated truck.

The Georgia border had been a welcome relief. The Mutaween would range a few miles past the state line to pursue her, she was sure, but they wouldn't dare go much farther for fear of running into a contingent of Georgia Militia. The Fedvamps spent as much time hunting the militia as the Mutaween did fighting the street gangs vying to supply Chattanooga with contraband. Taggart's strategy was generally to avoid all of them and let them fight each other while she slipped in and out.

She might have gotten back sooner if she hadn't insisted on hard coin. Aziz had tried to pay her in federal scrip, but everyone knew the Brasov Dollar was worthless. The Federal Reserve printed millions of them every day. It was the reason for the runaway inflation the country was suffering — to say nothing of the burgeoning black market that kept Taggart in shoes and go-hol.

Business had been a little *too* good, lately. Taggart's weapons shipments had picked up as the Georgia Militia stockpiled arms in anticipation of Brasov's crackdown on the state. Georgia was, officially, in non-compliance with the Emergency Powers Act, not to mention the decades-old ban on "military-style" semi-automatic firearms and "assault weapons." Federal aid had been cut off to the state in reprisal for the governor's refusal to enforce Brasov's executive orders. Only the Sharia enclaves still received regular infusions of tax dollars.

In addition to the Fedvamp patrols, Brasov had begun using government drones to launch air strikes against members of the Georgia state government. Authorization for the use of Scythe drones in American airspace, and against those Americans classified as seditionists or terrorists, had been part of the Emergency Powers Act. The result had been a brisk business in everything from rocket-propelled grenades to whatever Stingers she could scare up. Stingers were rare. So were LAWS rockets.

Thomas Simpson was a major backer of the Resistance and a frequent sponsor of her "gratis" deliveries to the rebels and the militia. Over the years he had paid for hundreds of Kalashnikovs and tens of thousands of rounds of ammunition for them. She knew she had a friend in him, and one she could trust to protect her from the Basij patrols. She just had to get to his property and she could breathe a little easier.

She was several hundred yards short of Simpson's property when the engine finally wheezed its last. The dash computer went berserk, displaying a dozen different warning lights and diagrams. From somewhere deep within the dash, the automation center tried to warn her that the drive train was seriously out of spec. Its synthesized voice was unintelligible. The truck was dead.

"Damn it," she said.

The vehicle was not registered to her; its multiple license transponders were all forgeries, stolen or retasked from other vehicles. Even the prepaid toll account that was debited whenever the vehicle traveled federal roads had been set up under another name. She had no fear that the truck would be traced to her. But she hated losing it. Trucks weren't cheap, and neither was the tank of the ethanol she was leaving behind. Perhaps Simpson could lend her a vehicle and a fuel tank so she could, preferably after dark, circle back and siphon what was left.

She managed to get the truck onto the side of the road and into the dubious cover of a cluster of trees near the shoulder. Slinging her pack and her Thompson over one shoulder, she climbed down and checked both ways before following the packed-earth road. The road had been graded not too long ago. It made for quick going. With the weapon over her shoulder, however, she was keenly aware of the fact that this was broad daylight. Getting caught with an automatic weapon by Fedvamps or the Basij meant an on-the-spot execution. Of course, the penalty for getting caught with a single-shot .22 or a pump-action shotgun were just as bad. Inside the enclaves, non-Muslims were forbidden to own "offensive weapons." Everywhere that was not an enclave was nominally subject to the federal Right To Safety laws, which had outlawed firearms years ago.

She stuck close to the tree line as she made her way down the dirt road paralleling the Simpson estate, ready to jump into the cover of the low hanging branches. She heard nothing on the road. Finally, she made her way to the base of the stone wall that delineated Simpson's property. It was overgrown with brush and crawling vines, which bespoke Simpson's age and health. There was a time, during their business relationship, that he had paid meticulous care to the grounds and the structures on them.

The smell of smoke was heavy now. She could not see the black cloud beyond the trees overhead, but she could hear the crackle of the fuel, the roaring of a bonfire. Was one of Simpson's outbuildings on fire?

She began scrambling up the wall. There were toe-holds where the stone sections met. Careful not to cut herself or snag her clothing on the broken glass jutting from the top of the wall, she began to lever herself up and over.

This far out, a fire could burn unchecked for hours before a water detail could be organized. Infrastructure like fire departments — or anything receiving federal subsidies and funding — had suffered in the face of Georgia's defiance. The Georgia Militia had itself begun trying to enlist and organize loosely structured volunteer firefighters, but they had a long way to go yet. If Thomas Simpson's home were on fire, it could very well burn to the ground before anyone could—

She stopped short at the sight of the man with the automatic weapon.

He was tall and powerfully built. Over his shoulder was slung, almost casually, a MAC-11 submachinegun. In his left hand he held a torch, which still smoldered. The heat from the bonfire before him was turning the grass brown at his feet. He, or someone else, had already dug a circle in the ground around the bonfire, to prevent the burning grass from spreading outward to the rest of the estate.

The wind shifted. The awful stench hit her full in the face. Once you had smelled it, you could never forget it. She knew that odor and the death it portended.

It was burning flesh.

Almost by reflex, she reached for her Thompson. The man at the bonfire turned to her. Only then did she the tears streaming down his face. He shook his head.

"Don't," he told her. "You don't have to."

There was something in his voice that she could not identify. She could not imagine why, but she left her Thompson over her shoulder. The man at the fire did not raise his weapon. Instead, he took a step back from the fire, held out his hand, and beckoned to her.

"Inside," he said. "I don't know how much time we have. We don't want to be caught out here."

She followed him through a rear door to the sprawling manor-house. Once inside, her boot hit something slick. She looked down.

There was blood everywhere.

He stopped her, then, as she tried to haul the Thompson down from her shoulder and bring it to bear. His grip was incredibly strong but, as they struggled in silence, he did not crush her wrist or forearm. He simply held her immobile. His grip was cool, almost refreshing after the heat of the bonfire.

"You're a vampire," she told him.

"My name is Vincent Harden," he said. "Thomas... Thomas Simpson was my friend."

Was. The significance of the word cut through her shock at the grisly scene around her. "The fire," she said. "That was for *Thomas*?"

Harden nodded. He looked down at the blood on the floor, then to the track she had made through it with her boot. "It isn't his, if that's what you're thinking," he said. He pointed. "Arturo and I struggled for this." He gestured with the MAC-11. "I managed to drop most of a magazine into him while we fought for the weapon."

"Thomas' Guy Friday? *That* Arturo?" she asked. "What the hell is going on here?"

"Easy," Harden said. He made his way into the kitchen, beckoning for her to follow. Once there, he did not sit so much as he collapsed into one of the high-backed chairs at the surprisingly modern kitchen island. Stainless steel and cast iron pots and pans hung above his head.

"He was tired," said Harden. "So tired of it all. He asked me to help him end it. He was my oldest and closest friend." Harden looked at his hands, which were smudged with soot and smeared with dried blood. "I built the pyre myself. He deserved that. He deserved an honorable burning. And it had to be now. She'll be coming."

"'She?' *Who's* coming?"

"You're... You're Tag Jones, aren't you?" Harden said.

"My friends call me Tag," she said. "I don't know *you* yet."

"Thomas spoke of you more than once," said Harden. He was still staring at his hands. "He had a lot of respect for you."

"You said we don't have much time," Tag reminded him. "Why? What were you talking about?"

"Elizabeth Hawkins," Harden spat. He said the name with so much venom that Tag almost started. "Arturo was her plant. Her eyes and ears here at the estate. And Thomas *knew* it. He entrusted his security to the man knowing that Hawkins wanted him alive, *needed* him alive for the scapegoat he represented. It's one of the reasons he allowed himself to die. And I guarantee he was funneling misinformation to Hawkins through Arturo for years. He was always so smart about these things. Patient. I don't know how we're going to see this through without him."

"See *what* through?"

"The Resistance," said Harden. "The fight against Brasov. That's what Thomas wanted. He wanted to see Brasov defeated. He recorded a video..." Harden stopped. He turned to Tag as if suddenly realizing something. "Even

.

31

that he planned. He *knew* the video was more powerful as a deathbed confession. He gave his life to give us that weapon."

"So what now?" Tag asked.

Harden glared, suddenly. She watched the change come over his face. He was shaking off the blow that was Thomas Simpson's death. The shock was falling away, to be replaced by something else. The strength in him was almost frightening, once his eyes were fixed on hers.

"Why are you here?" he said. "How did you get in?"

She grabbed for her weapon yet again, but he was on her with inhuman speed, pushing her up against the stainless steel oven built into the wall behind her. The cords of his arms were like steel. She struggled in his grip, the Thompson pinned behind her on its sling.

"Are you with *her*?" he demanded. "Are you working for Hawkins? ARE YOU WORKING FOR HAWKINS?"

His breath was strangely cool on her face; his lips were inches from hers. She fought a flush of terror and something else. "No," she managed. "My... my truck broke down. I was making a run and got caught up with the Mutaween. The truck was damaged. This was the closest safe haven."

He wasn't convinced. "Hawkins was monitoring Thomas through Arturo," he said. "She'll know he's dead. He hit me hard enough to daze me, put me down, and used the opportunity to escape. His wounds couldn't be fatal. He'd have waited out there somewhere long enough to heal and become more mobile. By now he's reported to Hawkins what took place. Her people will be on their way. Your arrival is convenient."

"I swear," she said. Her heart hammered in her chest. She tried to move and could not; he was like a statue. "I climbed the wall and found you. I'm with the Resistance. I hate Brasov as much as you do, as much as Thomas did. I'm on *your* side, Harden."

"You don't know me," he said, using her words. "You should get out of here while you can." He looked down at the MAC-11 and pulled its bolt back, checking it. "Leave before Hawkins arrives."

"I won't get far," she protested. "My truck is dead."

"Thomas has an old Jaguar parked in the drive," he said. "The keys will be under the visor. Take it. He would want a friend to have it. Take whatever else you need, if you can carry it. It won't matter. I've got to find a way to destroy the rest before I can go. Thomas wouldn't want his estate to become one of the People's Sharia Palaces. I'll have to see to it that it doesn't."

"What about you?" Tag asked.

"Thomas was like my father," Harden said. "'Stand your ground,' he said to me. 'Refuse to comply. Die on your feet.' His last wish was to fight Brasov to a standstill, to remove the cancer that man represents. That's what I'm going to do. But first I'm going to settle a score."

She realized, then. "Hawkins," she said. "You're going to wait for her, aren't you?"

"It's the first opportunity I'll have had for... Well. In a long time. I'm going to kill her."

"You said she was sending forces," Tag countered. "You'll be outnumbered. One vampire against many. You can't win against those odds."

"I can try," said Harden.

"You can't fight Brasov if Hawkins kills you!" Tag shouted, surprised by her own passion. "How is that different than Thomas letting himself die?"

Harden released her, suddenly. Her knees almost buckled. He turned away from her and, before she realized what he was doing, he had brought one fist down on the kitchen island. The marble cracked under the powerful blow.

"She has to pay."

"You've waited this long," Tag said, guessing. "Let me help you. I can get us to Van Gogh, the Resistance leader. We can figure out the next best step in the war against Brasov. I've talked to him a few times in the last two months. Shipments of arms have picked up. *Way* up. The Resistance is planning something big. If you want to honor Thomas' sacrifice, now is the time to do it."

Harden grimaced. Finally, he nodded. "All right. My car is parked behind Thomas' Jaguar. You drive that. I'll follow you. It won't hurt to have two vehicles, especially if we need to sell or barter the Jag. They command a premium these days, what with the British embargo and all."

Tag nodded. "Meet me in the driveway?"

"Yes," said Harden. "There are some things I need to gather up."

Tag hurried through the corridors of Simpson's estate, making her way toward the front and the circular drive. She saw plenty of things along the way that looked valuable. Simpson had decorated or accumulated in his home any number of antiques. The walls bore weapons that were equally as ancient, including an entire display of Civil War era swords and firearms. None of it looked like anything she would want to take with her.

How difficult would it be to burn down this house? If Tag knew Thomas Simpson at all, that could well mean he had rigged the estate to burn down. Incendiary grenades placed around the building? That was how she would do it. Better to torch it than let it fall to government seizure, would be his logic. She could not disagree.

Since the governments of the Sharia Enclaves had been empowered, like the Fedvamps, to seize properties owned by "seditionists" and "terrorists," a surprising number of valuable homes, cars, boats, and other property had been taken from suspected criminals. She supposed it was even possible that a couple of those arrests had actually been of Resistance sympathizers, but more often than not, the property seizures were conducted to enrich those enforcing them.

What a terrible shame to see a house this beautiful destroyed. It was almost as terrible as the loss of Simpson himself. He had been dedicated to the ideal of liberty. She would miss him. He had always reminded her of her grandfather... though, to be fair, Simpson was old enough that he could have been her grandfather's grandfather and then some. He had never admitted to her his precise age, but he had seen history that would now be lost with his passing. That, too, was a shame.

The Jaguar was a silver model, one of the last to be imported to the United States before the British embargo was enforced. Since the UK had fallen from within to Muslim rule, the British caliphate had demanded full compliance with Sharia doctrine in all its trading partners and military allies. The United States was not in compliance, claimed the Brits, because the Resistance had not yet been crushed. The thought actually amused her. It had to be a thorn in Brasov's side. Anything that caused that bastard difficulty was a good thing.

She was twenty feet from the Jaguar when it exploded.

She actually saw the smoke trail from the rocket propelled grenade that detonated the vehicle. The explosion of the grenade was followed, a fraction of a heartbeat later, by the eruption of the vehicle's fuel tank. A wave of heat and pressure smacked her bodily to the ground. She struck her head painfully on the pavement of the circular drive.

They were here. Hawkins and her zealots were here.

Elizabeth Hawkins' reputation was well deserved. While she did not command the strength the Cousinry boasted, she had significant numbers. The vampires who followed her were fiercely loyal, members of a cult of personality that venerated her for her beauty, her intelligence, and her ferocity. Rumors had long swirled that Hawkins held her group's loyalty with the liberal dispensing of sexual favors, but Tag had never believed that. You couldn't command the respect and loyalty of any group if they were passing you around like the town harlot.

More likely, Hawkins' considerable appeal was shared with select members of her command structure. That would ensure loyalty among those who could enforce it in others. And then, too, there was the fact that some vampires simply did not agree with either the Cousinry's ideals or Brasov's omnipotent-government approach. They preferred the selective elitism, the cultivated menace, of Hawkins' camp.

Tag realized that her mind was wandering. She was lying on her back, looking up at the sky. The pain in her spine told her that the Thompson was still with her. She dragged it from behind her shoulder, pulled the bolt back, and struggled to a sitting position. The ringing in her ears was the only thing she could hear. The explosion had been that close.

"Jones! Jones!" She heard the words as if through a tunnel far away. It was Harden, calling to her. As she turned, felling the heavy, murky disorientation, she began to hear the distant pops and cracks of small arms fire. It seemed much more distant than it was. But the ringing in her head was fading. The gunfire was growing louder.

A piece of asphalt jumped from the drive and struck her leg. Then it happened again. Then a larger piece of the driveway exploded near her right hip.

Gunfire. She was taking gunfire.

"JONES!" Harden was screaming. "The house! Run!"

She tried to stand. She was unsteady on her feet. Then a strong arm was around her waist, propelling her forward, turning her and rushing her back to the house. It was Harden. As he whisked her along, he fired the MAC-11 back the way they had come. Hot brass struck the pavement.

Clutching her Thompson, trying to shake off the effects of the blast, she struggled to bring the weapon up, to aim it at the front gate of the estate.

"No time for that!" Harden was yelling. "We've got to get to cover!"

"What is it?" she asked, wondering if her voice sounded as odd to him as it did to her. "What's happening?"

Harden turned and pointed. As he did so, the front gate was smashed in two. The armored personnel carrier that burst through the opening and rolled over the fallen gates was painted in a night camouflage pattern of black and gray tiger stripes. A single figure was visible in the open hatchway at the top of the APC.

Elizabeth Hawkins had come calling.

Chapter Five

Tag let Harden usher her back into the kitchen area. He took her to hide in the lee of the kitchen island, which had been hewn of granite and polished. It was thick and sturdy and would stop bullets; most of the walls of the house would not. External walls, interior walls… even in a house this old, built before modern, commercial construction techniques turned everything to cheap fiberboard, there was no real protection from rifle rounds.

Her professional mind identified the sound of the weapons even as she stole a glance through one of the cracked and broken kitchen windows. Harden dragged her back down behind the island. He was loading a fresh magazine into the MAC-11. Over his shoulder he now wore an olive-drab canvas messenger bag that looked thick and heavy with gear. He saw her looking and nodded.

"They've got AK100 series rifles," said Tag. "Probably surplus government issue, and plenty of them."

"I've got Arturo's extra magazines," Harden said, nodding. "And some weapons of my own. Keep that Thompson handy. They're coming a lot faster than I thought they would."

"We're completely outgunned. What are we going to do?" Tag asked, wishing she didn't sound as unnerved as she felt.

"We're going to wait," said Harden.

Bullets pocked the wall behind them, raining plaster dust on them and the kitchen island. The fire outside intensified, but it was unfocused. Hawkins' forces were peppering the house just to see what they could shake loose. The thought of all this waste, of all of Thomas' things torn apart for no reason but Hawkins' greed for power, stoke the flames of Harden's anger.

"We've got to get to the Cobra," said Harden.

"They'll be setting up a perimeter," said Tag. Harden looked at her, his expression appraising. *That's right*, Tag thought. *I know how these games are played.*

Harden set about checking his own weapons. He had a pair of Commander-length .45 automatics in Kydex holsters behind either hip. He checked each in turn before replacing them. The MAC-11 he had already tested under fire; he knew it would work. Arturo had very thoughtfully left behind a stack of thirty-round magazines — enough that Harden's war bag, already laden with the fire safe and several other items, was uncomfortably heavy.

Rounds continued to pop and ricochet over their heads. Several rounds struck the heavy iron stove in the corner, becoming angry metal bees as they spalled off in random directions. Tag felt one of the rounds strike the floor near her foot. She drew her leg up under her, hugging the heavy kitchen island closer.

"We can't stay here," said Tag.

Harden peered up over their shelter. He ducked back down almost immediately. "They're not close enough," he said. "I need them to move in. But it wouldn't hurt to have some additional cover. Some more chaos to obscure our run to the car."

"Any suggestions?"

"Thomas kept a storeroom at the opposite end of the house. It's at the end of the long corridor, on the left."

"I've seen it," she said.

"He'll have smoke grenades there. I didn't think to grab any. There were more important things to take." He patted the canvas bag.

There's also a couple of LAWS rockets, if I remember correctly," she said. "I've helped Thomas stock that room many a time."

Harden looked thoughtful. "We could do with one."

"Then there's your answer," she said.

"Wait here," said Harden. "Pop off a few rounds with your Thompson. Doesn't matter if you hit anything. I'll go for the storeroom."

"Uh uh," she said, shaking her head. "I'm the one that hauled that gear in there. I bet I visited Thomas a lot more than you did. If anybody's going to find what we need, it should be me."

"You're not bulletproof."

"Neither are you," said Tag. "Not... really. You're just more stubborn about dying from them. Let me go. I can handle it."

"All right," said Harden. He didn't look happy, but he also seemed to understand there was no point arguing with her. "Let me cover you. On three. One. Two."

"Three!" shouted Tag, and ran for all she was worth.

She could hear Harden swearing behind her. He poured on the nine millimeter fire from the MAC-11, spraying the window in the direction of Hawkins' troops. More rounds zinged through the hall before and behind her, but she kept running, ducking and weaving, hoping it would make a difference.

She supposed she should be grateful. Hawkins' people could be human or they could be vampire — there was always a human entourage where vampires gathered, unless they were Cousinry personnel — but they were attacking a Cousinry facility as far as they knew. Thomas and Harden were vampires, so throwing tear gas into the building was a pointless gesture. Tag was glad of that; she hated tear gas.

The storage room was locked. It had an old electronic combination lock and she could not, for the life of her, remember Thomas' most recent code. He changed it regularly, so there was no guarantee it would work even if she knew it. Several fat, slow-moving .45 rounds made short work of the jamb around the lock. It was enough for her to pry it open after burning through most of a magazine.

Thomas. She could hardly believe he was gone. It did not seem real to her, any more than this firefight and the other vampire, Harden, seemed real. He as handsome enough, if distant. She could tell that Hawkins' name alone was enough to make him furious. She'd seen that in men before. The set of the jaw, the way his hands clenched. The white knuckles that spoke of control, barely maintained.

He's not a man, she reminded herself. *He's a Cousinry vampire.*

She found the crate of smoke grenades and a small duffel bag into which to throw them. The bag was full of instant rations — dehydrated packets attacked to compressed water cylinders that, at the thumb of a tab, could be reconstituted. She had to dump some of those to accommodate the grenades, but it seemed wise to have some food with them. There was no telling how long they might be on the run… if they got to the Cobra at all, much less off the estate.

First things first.

There was a single LAWS rocket tube. She took this too. Whatever Thomas had done with the other Light Anti-tank Weapons System she had sold him, she could not say. The weapons had commanded a very high price, and rightly so. Heavy ordnance was becoming harder and harder to come by. Good as business was, what would she do if the supply ran out? What would *any* of them do if they couldn't fight back?

The gunfire outside stopped abruptly. In the strange silence that followed, Tag hurried back along the corridor, positioning herself once more behind the granite island with Harden. He looked at her, his face creased with disgust.

"What?" she asked.

Harden jerked his chin toward the shattered window. Tag risked yet another look from the edge of the island; Hawkins had removed her helmet with its smoked visor and was now standing atop the APC. Her gray striped fatigues had been fitted to her figure. Tag did not like to admit that she looked devastatingly sexy, posing like that with a Glock pistol in one gloved fist. In her other hand she held a compact megaphone.

"Vincent Harden," Hawkins' amplified voice was loud enough to reach them clearly in the kitchen. "I know you're in there. Come out and you won't be killed."

Tag looked at Harden. His fist was turning white on the sheet-metal grip of the MAC-11.

She wasn't sure, but she thought she heard him say under his breath, "Get stuffed."

"Vincent Harden," said Hawkins again. "The estate is surrounded. There is nowhere for you to go. I'm not asking much. Just leave this place. Leave the house intact. Leave all of Thomas' papers and personal effects. Leave now and fight another time… or I stake you out on the south lawn and we'll wait for the sunrise together."

"She means it," said Tag softly. "She's known for—"

"*I know what she's known for,*" Harden hissed, his voice so hot that Tag had to back away. "I know. Better than most."

"This is your last warning," said Hawkins. "It's not going to go well for you, Harden. I will make it hurt. I will make your death last. And in the end you'll suffer every bit as much as—"

"Have you found Arturo?" Harden bellowed. "He wasn't looking too good last I saw him."

"Arturo," said Hawkins through the megaphone, "will be rewarded for his service."

"I hear you like to dole out rewards," called Harden. "Honestly I'm amazed you don't walk funny, what with all the loyalty you inspire."

Hawkins raised her arm and fired a shot at the kitchen. She fired three more times before she managed to bring herself under control, but apparently it was all the distraction Harden needed or wanted. He held out his hand, his fingers grasping at the air, and Tag pulled the pin from a smoke grenade before giving it to him.

Harden stood and took a bullet in the shoulder. He grunted, but it was not his throwing side; he hurled the grenade. There was a hiss and a pop as the smoke grenade detonated. Soon, a pall of purple smoke was drifting across the front of Thomas Simpson's former home.

"Purple haze," said Harden quietly.

"What?" said Tag.

"Nothing," said Harden. He repeated the process several more times, thankfully avoiding getting shot. Soon the smoke was so thick outside that it was drifting back into the house through the shattered windows. Tag braced herself for what she assumed would be a run for the car, but Harden help up his hand. "No," he said. "Not yet."

Tag did not understand. "But we just went to all the trouble of making cover for ourselves," she said.

"It's not for us," said Harden. "Not yet. It's for them."

"But—"

"Don't trust me," said Harden. "Trust Thomas. He knew this day would come. 'Something special,' he said. 'You'll know.' Those were his words. I found the special something taped to his fire safe."

"What?" said Tag.

Harden held up a remote detonator. He flicked its activator switch, priming the circuit.

Tag's eyes widened.

"Thomas was smart," said Harden. "He was the smartest man I've ever known. And he liked to plan ahead. I think he must have known for years that Arturo, someone he was supposed to be able to trust, someone who owed him a blood debt, was working for Hawkins. I have his journal. It's possible he discloses in it when Arturo turned against him. I won't know until I read it. But he used that knowledge against Hawkins. He had to have. I'm willing to bet he was feeding Hawkins misinformation for longer than any of us would think possible. It's the kind of man Thomas was."

"You have until the count of five!" Hawkins said through her megaphone. "All troops, move in! On my mark, breach the house and kill everyone inside it!"

"There it is," said Harden. "Guess we're out of time."

She saw the look in his eyes. He was angry, yes. But he was also… pained. Disappointed.

"One!" shouted Hawkins.

"What is it?" said Tag. "What's wrong?" *Beyond the obvious, I mean*, she thought. *Beyond the fact that we're surrounded by a hostile rogue vampire force that wants to kill you and would do God knows what to me.*

"Two!" called Hawkins.

"I'm not going to be able to get her," said Harden. "There are too many. There won't be time to deal with them, get away, and also pause to take her head."

"This is a surprise to you?" asked Tag.

"Three!" shouted Hawkins. "Four!"

"No," said Harden. "Just a shame. Just a damned shame."

"Fi—" started Hawkins.

"Five," whispered Vincent Harden, and squeezed the trigger on the remote detonator.

The house shook. From outside, the screams of Hawkins' vampire troops were more than inhuman. They were… obscene. Tag had never heard anything like it. She never wanted to again.

The noises that had preceded the explosions were hollow, pneumatic. Those would be tubes for two-stage antipersonnel devices. Thomas has once had a conversation with Tag about them, but she'd never thought he would actually go through with it. It must have taken tremendous effort to make it work.

"Bouncing Betties," said Tag quietly. The explosions continued outside, as did the screaming. The sound was moving farther away from the house. Of course; that made sense. Thomas would have rigged the charges to explode closest to the house first, then in stages in an ever widening perimeter, chasing after a retreating foe.

"Land mines?" asked Harden.

"No," said Tag. "A theoretical anti-vamp Bouncing Betty. Thomas quizzed me on the mechanics of it, wanted to know what munitions I could get for him. White phosphorous and shards of wood. Heat-activated, acid-coated round shot for added kick. It's an anti-vampire cocktail. It probably won't kill them, but it's going to make them wish it had."

Harden nodded. "Come on," he said, grabbing her hand.

They made their way through the wreckage of the bullet-pocked house and to the garage. The fire from Thomas' Jaguar had scorched the paint of the Cobra, but if Harden noticed, he did not react. He held her door for her and she piled in. Stowing his gear behind his seat, keeping the MAC-11 close, he jumped behind the steering wheel and fired up the old car. The engine offered a throaty growl, a power Tag had not experienced in an automobile. When Harden threw the beast in drive, it almost threw them sideways as he burned rubber out of the garage.

The scene outside the house was charnel. The bodies on the blood-soaked lawn of Simpson's estate were largely immobile; many of them were probably human. A few twitched, here and there, either wounded and not dead, or undead and slowly recovering. It would not matter. By the time any vampires among them were mobile again, they would be long gone.

Harden slowed as they passed the blood-streaked APC. Tag found herself wondering: Would Hawkins be there? Could she have ducked inside the vehicle to avoid the mines? Tag could tell that Harden wanted to stop, wanted to search among the bodies for her, but the danger would be too great. There was no telling if Hawkins had summoned reserve forces. If they wanted to get clear of a possible second wave, while avoiding taking a bullet or a blade in the back from some staggering rogue vampire regaining his senses, they had to get well clear. Every principle of warfare Tag had learned with the Resistance told her that much.

"She's dead, probably," Tag said.

"No," said Harden. "I would know. I would... feel it. Somehow. She's still in this world. Nearby, too. But I can't have her today. Not today."

"She'll be pretty ripped up," said Tag. "If she was exposed during that blast, Thomas' weapons won't have done her any favors. She could be permanently scarred."

Harden's lip curled up. It was a cruel smile, the smile of a killer. The moment passed quickly, but the viciousness that had flashed across Harden's face... it was nothing like he seemed. She could only assume that was what his obvious hatred for Elizabeth Hawkins brought out in him.

Harden leaned into the steering wheel and shifted. The Cobra surged forward into the night.

"Good," was all he said.

Chapter Six

Georgia, 1956

"Vincent."

Harden struggled to wake. Sleep. He needed to sleep. He was so tired.

"Vincent. Vincent!"

When he finally managed to open his eyes, Harden found himself staring at Jacob Muller, one of Thomas' human lieutenants, an ally to the Cousinry. Muller had been attached to Thomas' estate for close to thirty years.

"What happened?"

"Are you hurt?" Jacob asked. He was a gaunt man; some men grew fat in their older age, while others grew thin. Jacob was the latter. He survived on a diet of hard work, coffee, and donuts, from what Harden could see.

"I'm not... I'm okay, Jacob." He felt at his scalp. His fingers came away bloody, but not too badly. The wound was closing. Suddenly, he remembered. "Thomas? Is Thomas okay?"

"He's safe," said Jacob. "You stopped her. You stopped the attack."

Harden sat up and the barn swam around him. He felt fuzzy. Though the open doors he could see that twilight was falling now, which would make it easier for him to move around. His large-brimmed hat was lying on the floor of the barn next to him.

The sprawling pecan farm, 25 acres across Northeast Georgia, had been his home for more than a century. It would become two before he knew it. In all this time, he had found his place in the world; he had found a measure of peace and satisfaction. Thomas, and the Cousinry, were not far away. Times were reasonably good. For Harden, it was enough.

But now he smelled smoke.

"What is—" he started to stand.

"Wait," said Jacob, holding him by the arm. The spindly man was no match for Harden's strength, but something in Jacob's eyes stopped the vampire cold.

"What is it?"

"It's... Vincent, it's the kennels. Hawkins people burned them."

Harden felt his jaw twitch. "How many?"

"All of them," said Jacob. "I'm sorry, Vincent. We were too late to save any. We came back as soon as Thomas was secure, but... Hawkins' people must have been so angry that you foiled her kidnap attempt that she left you a message she knew would hurt you."

Harden suppressed a sigh. There was no point in letting it anger him. It did nonetheless; he was furious. Harden was known locally for the Dobermans he raised here on the farm. It was how he had met Cordelia, in fact. One of his animals had been having difficulty whelping and Harden, unable to reach his usual veterinarian, had ridden out to the edge of Gatlinburg in his old Ford on Thomas' recommendation. Cordelia and her teenage daughter, Marlena, had come back to the farm with him. Harden had not known then that he would fall in love with Cordelia, who was then a widow. He did not know that he would come to love Marlena as his own daughter. But he had.

He was drifting. The blow to the head, more than likely. The concussion would clear in a few more minutes. He was forgetting something—

"Cordelia," he said. "Marlena. Are they safe?"

The look on Jacob's face told him they were not. "Hawkins took them," he said. "That was her message, Vincent." He held out his hand. In it was a scrap of white fabric. Harden's eyes narrowed. The scrap of clothe looked like it had come from Cordelia's blouse. On it, scrawled in dried blood, were three words: *Gaitlinsberg road house.*

"I need my guns," said Harden.

"You were in the sun all day," said Jacob. "You fought half a dozen of Hawkins' loyalists. Vampires, all of them, Vincent. You're in no condition to go anywhere."

"I said I need my guns," Vincent hissed. Jacob started. His eyes grew wide. Then he nodded. "All right, my friend," he said, relenting. "All right. But you broke your saber fighting today. You'll need another blade."

"Find me something," said Harden. "An axe, a machete. Anything. But hurry."

"Yes, Vincent," said Jacob. "Right away."

* * *

The Ford coughed and wheezed its way down the dirt road to Gaitlinsberg. Harden drove with the lights off. His eyes, like the eyes of all vampires, were light-sensitive. He could see in the dark as well as most men could see during the day. There would be almost no traffic on the road at this time of night. Gaitlinsberg drew locals from the opposite direction, in Morrow, but there was little moving on the other side.

Harden's WWII-issue 1911 pistols were tucked in his belt behind his hips. He had thrown a map case of extra magazines over his shoulder. On the seat next to him was a rusty fire axe on which Jacob had filed a hasty edge. Harden did not know if it would be enough, but he hoped so.

Thomas had been visiting Vincent at the pecan farm when Hawkins' people made their play. There had been no time even to get his weapons. Harden had time only to reach his saber, which hung on the wall over the door of his home. He had fought his way savagely through

There would be no choice but to kill Hawkins and as many of her people as he could. That was the only way to prevent them from attempting another kidnapping of Thomas. Hawkins had long been a thorn in the side of the Cousinry, but seldom was she this bold; her questionable legal status in both the human and vampire worlds usually kept her in check. It had long worried Thomas that her power seemed to be growing. The older vampire had told Harden many times that it would be necessary to make a bold statement in order to put her back in her place.

But now Harden was going to kill her.

She had struck at his home. She had murdered his dogs. None of that mattered because Thomas had been ushered to safety by Cousinry allies among Harden's staff at the farm. But Hawkins, ever the sore loser, had taken Cordelia and Marlena. If either of them had been hurt, Harden would make Hawkins suffer to her last breath. Even if they were unharmed, he intended to kill her. He would not permit her to endanger those he loved ever again.

He was strangely calm about the prospect of murdering Elizabeth Hawkins. Harden had killed, yes. He did not remember all of their faces. It was war, after all, and while he felt the gravity of the lives he had taken, he believed in the cause. He believed in the Revolution and did not regret his actions. He had taken part in subsequent wars as well. He had taken more lives as a vampire than he had as a human, in fact, but as a man kills a man — not as a predator. He may not be human now, but he was not a monster. It was for these reasons that the ideals of the Cousinry spoke so strongly to him.

He was going to make Elizabeth Hawkins pay for what she had done. He was going to make it clear to all vampires that his family, this human woman and her daughter, were under his protection. He would show Hawkins loyalists that—

He barely had time to recognize the cinder block that struck his windshield.

* * *

Harden opened his eyes again. This time, his head was perfectly clear, although his head felt heavy. He could scarcely keep his neck up. Every inch of his body cried out for rest. Dried blood covered his clothes. It was his own blood.

His wrists and ankles hurt badly. He looked down and, in the light of a single bulb hanging from the ceiling, he could see that barbed wire had been used to strap him to the chair. He was very weak. The cumulative effects of sun exposure, the fighting he had done earlier, the wreck of the truck...

The truck. He remembered it rolling over and over again. He remembered feeling his bones crack and splinter. He had jerked the wheel coming around a tight corner of the dirt road as the cinder block struck him. The resulting accident would have torn apart a human being.

The room in which he sat was cramped. Shelves bearing canned goods reached from floor to ceiling. He smelled a dozen different aromas. They were pleasant smells, food smells. He was likely in the store room of the road house, a bar and grill outside Gaitlinsberg.

He could hear sounds. He could hear screaming. His heart leapt... until he realized it wasn't screaming. It was yelling. It was Elizabeth Hawkins yelling in rage. Furniture was being smashed. He heard cups and plates being broken.

That wasn't all he could hear. He wasn't alone. The door to the storage room was being shut. A human couldn't hear its hinges, but a vampire could. Thomas tensed.

"Mister Harden? Vincent?"

"Marlena?" Harden felt his jaw drop. "What are you doing here?"

It was Cordelia's beautiful seventeen-year-old daughter, looking more frightened than Harden had ever seen her. Her face was smudged with dirt and her sun dress was likewise soiled, but she seemed uninjured.

In her hands she held a pair of wire cutters.

"Mother needs your help," Marlena whispered.

"How are you here? What is happening?" he whispered back. Beyond the store room, beyond what he assumed was the kitchen of the road house, Hawkins' continued her destructive spree.

"That woman, that awful woman," said Marlena. "She's very upset."

"Why?"

"We got away," said Marlena. "She left us alone. Mother and I were tied up here with just one man... just one man to guard us. She went with the others to wait for you on the road and capture you. They mean to torture you, Mister Harden. I heard her speak of it."

"How did you get here?"

"I snuck back in," she said. "There's a back door in the kitchen. When the man was guarding us, he used wire to tie us up. Not sharp wire like yours. Just baling wire. I... I told him he could have me. The guard. I told him he could have me if he untied me. So he brought the cutters and he cut the wire and I when he put them down I picked them up and hit him and ran—"

"Slow down, Marly, slow down," Harden urged. "What about your mother? Where is your mother?"

"I think she's out *there*," said Marlena. "With the vampires and that woman. The guard was chasing me. I had to run away. There are woods behind this place. I circled back to get mother and snuck in. But instead of her, I found you."

Harden's mind reeled. The thought Marlena, at just seventeen, thinking to lure a guard with promises of access to her body... it turned his stomach.

She was brave. Braver than any one he'd seen, short of her mother. She reminded him so much of his own children.

She was cutting the wires from his wrists and ankles. Without the bonds holding him in the chair, he collapsed to the floor. Marlena tensed, probably wondering if anyone had heard the noise. But Hawkins' temper tantrum had not abated. Something large and heavy hit the floor beyond the kitchen. It might have been a table being smashed.

"I can't," Harden whispered. "Marlena... I'm too weak."

Her wrist appeared before him. "Drink my blood," she said simply.

Harden tried to recoil. "No," he said softly. "I won't. I won't do it."

"They'll catch me," said Marlena. "There's no way I can sneak out of here again. And they'll come back and kill you, Mister Harden. Drink my blood. Take just what you need. I'll be okay."

Harden hadn't fed from a human for more than a century. But the girl was right. If there was a chance to save Cordelia...

Marlena jumped as Harden's fangs pierced her wrist.

* * *

Elizabeth Hawkins, panting, arranged her tight-fitting sweater. The black leather gloves on her hands were stiffening as the blood on them dried. At her feet, the human fool she had trusted to guard Harden's bitch looked up at her with wide, dead eyes. His hands were still wrapped around the table leg with which she'd impaled him.

Around her, the wreckage of the road house was testimony to her rage. Not a stick of furniture was untouched. Her vampires looked at each other, holding their shotguns and hunting rifles loosely. None of them dared bring himself to her attention when she was in one of these black moods.

The woman — what was her name, Cordelia? — sat on the floor in the corner. She had been bound and gagged with a bandanna and a length of baling wire. But then, so had the daughter, and that stood to ruin everything.

Harden, right now, would be unconscious. That was no good. She needed his body to heal from the injuries it had sustained in the crash. She needed him healthy enough so that she could torture him. He was Thomas Simpson's golden boy, after all. Torturing him to death and leaving him buried to his neck in the front yard would go a long way towards teaching Thomas what it meant to foil her plans. Who knows? Simpson had become increasingly sentimental in recent years. The loss of his adopted vampire son might well break him.

Torturing Harden would be so much easier with the daughter. Men were always very sentimental about their lovers, but a child... an innocent child, put to the blade or to open flame in front of Harden's eyes, would drive the bastard to depths of agony. And now, thanks to one simpering human fool, one idiot who could not contain his urges, that was ruined—

Her vampire ears heard the hinges of the door to the kitchen. Some among her team, a mix of human and vampires, should have heard it too. The man holding a pump-action twelve-gauge and standing nearest the kitchen did not. The human fool probably died never understanding that Vincent Harden had rammed a pair of wire cutters into his throat.

The shotgun blasts that filled the room walked ever closer to Hawkins herself. Two of her vampires were struck in the neck. One was nearly decapitated. It was Vincent Harden, his eyes burning with hate, and he knew just how to use the weapon to its greatest advantage in the close quarters of the road house. A blast caught her in the shoulder and spun her, the pellets burning as they ripped open her flesh. She tried to reach for her own gun. Her gun hand felt dead. It would be useless until her flesh knit...

Harden paused and used the butt of the shotgun like a club. He crushed the skull of the last of her human soldiers and then aimed the weapon in her direction. The enraged vampire still had blood trailing from the corners of his mouth.

Harden jacked the pump back, then forward.

Hawkins snarled and threw herself out the nearest window.

* * *

"She's right in here," said Harden.

Cordelia breathed a sigh of relief. But that sigh turned into a scream when she entered the store room.

Harden gasped. Marlena was lying on the floor. Her eyes were closed and she was deathly pale.

"No, no, no," Harden whispered. He rushed to Marlena's side and cradled her in his arms. She whimpered but was turning colder by the second. "No, I couldn't have—"

"Vincent?" asked Cordelia. "What is it? What have they done to her?"

"It isn't what they've done," said Harden. He looked at her, his despair written on his face. "It's what I did. I haven't fed from a person in... I didn't know how much to take. I thought I stopped soon enough."

"Vincent?"

"I took too much," said Harden. "God help me, I took too much."

Chapter Seven

Outside Athens, Georgia

"They don't make them like this anymore," said Tag into the wind. The antique Shelby Cobra hummed along, pressing her back in her seat, faster than any smart-car she had ever been in. Most fascinating, the car didn't do anything for the driver. Harden had to control everything himself. As she watched, he reached down and manually shifted again. The car, impossibly, picked up even more speed.

The ride was rough. The road was not in good repair — few roads were, these days — but the Cobra, low-slung though it was, weaved in and out of the largest of the potholes. The fact that Harden was able to control the dinosaur of a vehicle as deftly as he did spoke to his great skill, especially because one of his hands was occupied with his phone. He held the sleek oblong of glass against his ear with his left hand, which meant there were moments when he didn't seem to be touching the steering wheel at all.

Tag shook her head. They didn't make them like Vincent Harden anymore, either. For starters, the man wore a wristwatch, an affectation she hadn't seen on anyone except a few very old, very wealthy men, or characters in movies and games. He might as well have a pocket watch on a gilded chain in his waistcoat. She knew nothing about watches, but Harden's was big, heavy, and looked like it had once been quite expensive. For as long as she could remember, since her childhood, everyone around her carried a clock, camera, video recorder, and calculator right in their phones. What purpose would a wristwatch serve?

Harden had made several calls. He had used what she thought were code-phrases with each of his calls, and the conversations seemed strangely stilted. She gathered he was making calls to other highly placed members of the Cousinry, telling them that Thomas Simpson was dead and that, Harden, had assumed the reins of the organization. Some of the conversations seemed to go better than others. Not everyone seemed to think Harden's new position was a good thing.

She had wanted to go straight to Van Gogh, but Harden insisted they needed to make a stop first near Athens. He had assured her it would be worth it. He had also taken the time, during a brief stop along the way near a pull-off in the trees, to show her some of the vehicle's hidden compartments. She would need to know where they were, Harden reasoned, if they were going to be relying on each other to stay alive. The implied compliment — and the implied possession — had given her a thrill she didn't know how to interpret.

Harden's Cobra held, concealed in its panels, a pair of United States government-issue .45 automatics that had to be close to a hundred years old. Another compartment held an even older double-edged sword with a cruciform guard. Still another held a modern military tomahawk, while the last held a vintage AK-47. It was the Kalashnikov she was admiring now, holding it low to keep it out of sight. It was concealed in a panel accessible to the passenger side, so anyone riding with the driver could provide fully automatic support.

Tag's own Thompson was stowed behind the back seat. She was very attached to the weapon, but she had always admired the beauty of the Kalashnikov-pattern rifles. She had certainly seen and sold enough of them, both vintage and modern reproductions, over the years.

Harden tucked the phone back in his shirt pocket. She took the opportunity to ask him the question that had been nagging at her. "How old is this AK?" she said.

"Vietnam," said Harden.

"What?" said Tag.

"Viet... Do you not know the Vietnam war?"

"When was it? Where was it?" She felt her face growing hot. Obviously, Harden felt this was something anybody would know. She didn't like feeling stupid.

"I forget that you're a product of modern government schools," said Harden, shaking his head. "You're so... *young*."

Tag flushed harder. She turned away so he wouldn't see. When she had regained control, she turned back and said, "So teach me."

"The second Indochina War," said Harden. "Say, 1955 to 1975 when Saigon fell."

"Saigon," said Tag. "You're talking about the Resistance War Against America in Southeast Asia."

"Is that what they call it now?" Harden said. He shook his head once more. "It shouldn't surprise me. Brasov and those like him have been twisting the education system for years, manipulating news and history to serve their interests. I'm willing to bet what you think you know about the history of this nation is fragmented at best, and composed of outright lies at worst. Kids today learn only what Brasov wants them to know. It's been that way since almost before you were born."

"So tell me about Brasov," said Tag. She looked behind her; there was no sign of surveillance or pursuit, which was good. Harden's car was not exactly low-profile. "Tell me what really happened to bring him to power."

"All right," said Harden. "President for Life Woodrow Brasov was the first admitted vampire to run for the presidency. We know the rumors, that Brasov might well be Vlad Tepes, or Vlad the Impaler. It's been whispered for long enough. But when Brasov first ran for office, he claimed to have been born in, and turned in, the United States. He ran as a Social Democrat, riding the tidal wave that swept the ultra-progressives into power just before the middle of the century. His Republican opponent was narrowly defeated. There was a lot of talk of voter fraud, and in truth, the Social Democrats had been rigging the vote for decades — starting with the federally mandated switch to electronic voting machines, manufactured by companies they controlled. They didn't stop there, though. The Social Democrats were fond of 'guarding' polling places, scaring away anyone whose skin was the wrong color or whose politics weren't correct."

"How would you vote if you didn't vote by machine?"

Harden looked at her, taking his eyes off the road for a minute. "Paper," he said. "Paper ballots. You've heard the phrase 'ballot box,' haven't you?"

"I guess I never thought about what that meant," said Tag.

"Most people don't," said Harden. "Most of us never think beyond our time. Tag, the only reason I know all this is because I lived long enough to see it."

"How old *are* you? Thomas never spoke of you. Yet I gather you two were very close."

"I fought with General Washington," said Harden.

"Washington... from Mount Brasov, *that* Washington?"

Harden grimaced. His jaw worked back and forth. "Yeah," he finally said. "Sort of." He swerved to avoid a pothole deep enough to break an axle had they driven into it. The government taxed citizens at rates higher than ever before, these days, but almost no funds were channeled to infrastructure. There were more pressing concerns, like funding reparations to Sharia enclaves and minority action groups, as well as increasing large sums paid to the government indoctrination programs that passed for schools.

"There are scratches in the stock of this rifle," said Tag. "Twenty-three of them, all in a row."

"The previous owner was keeping score," said Harden. "I took it from him."

Tag watched the scrub and trees go by for a while. "So what happened after Brasov was elected?" she finally prompted.

"Brasov's opponent committed suicide," said Harden. "That was the official account. It was a first in American politics. It wouldn't be the last. The Social Democrats had a fairly bad record where that was concerned already; anyone who caused them trouble had a nagging tendency to have a fatal accident, to turn up abruptly dead. One fellow, in particular, was found folded tightly enough to fit in a duffel bag that was left lying in his own bathtub. They declared *his* death a suicide, too, and of course the USB drive full of data incriminating Democrats in shady political deals was all lies.

"USB?"

"A memory card. Not important. Anyway, the Republicans cried foul and tried to sue in federal court for a recount. The courts had all been stacked by Democrats long before then; there was no way to get a fair ruling. The Republicans were overruled."

"I haven't heard the name 'Republicans' for a long time."

"That's because the party was banned thirty years ago," said Harden. "But I'm getting ahead of myself. Eighteen months into his presidency, Brasov had seen to it that key members of the Social Democrats had been turned, given eternal life as vampires. Once he had his power structure in place, he wrote the Emergency Executive Powers Act. The Social Democrats held Congress, the Senate, and the Presidency; they rammed it down our throats with little difficulty on a straight party-line vote. Then they set about gutting the First and Second Amendments to the Constitution. Please tell me you've read the Constitution. The original, not the Social Democrats' 'Constitution Two Point Oh.'"

"The Resistance passes out pocket Constitutions," said Tag. "I've read it. It's...depressing."

"It is now," said Harden. "Because as bad as we thought things were when Brasov and the Social Democrats established themselves as totalitarian rulers of what was once America, it was about to get a lot worse. Radical Islam, as it had since the beginning of the twenty-first century, continued to grow in power. Its adherents got bolder and bolder once Brasov made his sympathies clear. Thomas and the Cousinry discovered, even back then, that Brasov was working with a number of Islamist organizations. He wasn't just funding them privately and stating his support for them publicly. He was promising them parts of America."

"The Sharia enclaves," said Tag.

"Exactly so," said Harden. "He promised them — and ultimately delivered — control of large areas in several major cities. Detroit, and parts of Michigan, including what you know as Dearbornistan and Allah's New Hamtramck, fell first. Then New York, Chicago, Los Angeles... All of the largest progressive centers were ceded to the Muslims, in whole or in part. Sharia Law became the law of the land, and for non-Muslim law enforcement officers, the enclaves became no-go zones."

"Thomas spoke of the war between Islam and the Cousinry. I got the impression his servant, Arturo, had something to do with that."

"That's a story for another time," said Harden. "But yes. Like Hitler before him, Brasov orchestrated his own Night of the Long Knives. Hitler you know; he is often used, now, as an example of the 'right wing.' The Social Democrats conveniently forget that like them, Hitler was a socialist; he was a left-winger, not a member of the 'far right.' But regardless, Hitler had his *Sturmabteilung*, or SA. They were the street soldiers he used to intimidate his enemies and solidify his hold on power at the grassroots level. Brasov wanted an SA of his own, and he found it in the Islamists."

"The Mutaween?"

"The Basij are the shock troops now, yes," said Harden. "But back then, the Sharia patrol units weren't even on the drawing board. Back then, Brasov simply had hordes of loosely organized Muslims 'patrolling' the streets to do his bidding. It all started with his shock troops."

"The Fedvamps," supplied Tag.

"No, these are older," said Harden. "The Ottoman Turks used to maintain an elite infantry unit that formed the Ottoman Sultan's household troops and bodyguards. They were created by Sultan Murad the First in 1383. Janissaries, they were called. It's rumored that Brasov somehow had access to, and control over, a unit of Janissaries back then. It's not been discussed since; it's one of those topics that is deemed seditious, not to mention a violation of the Federal Leadership Criticism Act."

"But they were vampires," said Tag. "Vampires from the fourteenth century."

"Yes," said Harden. "Brasov sent his shock troops into the very Islamist enclaves he helped establish, two years after the first ones went up. Thousands of Muslims, most of them women and children, were slaughtered. Brasov went on national television and blamed the Cousinry. Said the Cousinry, clinging to outmoded and dangerously reactionary ideas of individualism, had orchestrated the killings in an attempt to 'send the dirty Muslims back where they came from.' Of course, the necessary evidence was manufactured and then widely disseminated. Brasov pledged his support to fight the Cousinry and cede even more United States territory to Sharia Law for the 'safety of our Muslim brothers and sisters, who worked so hard to build the backbone of this great nation.' Those were his exact words. I still remember them."

"And that's why the Mutaween, and the Caliphs running the enclaves, hate the Cousinry."

"That single night's work solidified Brasov's hold on the nation and guaranteed him the support of the Islamist voting bloc," said Harden. "It also gave him a scapegoat, a common enemy to use to rally people around his banner. Any time anything didn't go well, the Cousinry was somehow to blame. We were already trying to pick up the pieces after Elizabeth Hawkins and her supporters outed us to the world. This drove us even deeper into hiding."

"What does Hawkins want?"

"She always felt the Cousinry was an elite club that played by too many rules," explained Harden. "She believes vampires are superior to humans; we believe they are equals. She wants vampires to take their rightful place ruling the earth over humanity; we believe that's wrong. Her desire for vampires to become the ruling class of this planet is what prompted her, early on, to ally with Brasov. For reasons nobody's quite sure of, that didn't work out. My pet theory is that while she's an evil bitch and he's practically Satan incarnate, there's room for only one ruler in Social Democrat Hell."

"You might be holding in your feelings a little too much, Harden," said Tag without looking at him.

Harden shot her a glance. He turned back to the road without comment. Eventually, he said, "There's also the vast, hidden fortune the Cousinry manages."

"The what?" Tag said, startled.

"It was the primary purpose of the Cousinry," said Harden. "Sure, we acted as a buffer between humanity and vampires. We tried to keep the two out of each other's way while maintaining the secret of our existence. And we contributed where we could, always in secret, helping humanity along its path. But all that time, century after century, we were building wealth. Investing it. Channeling it. We have vast secret finances, a fortune that Hawkins wants to control. Thomas held a lot of other secrets, too, the kind of knowledge that comes from being among the few creatures who were alive to witness it as it happened... and to pass down the unique recordings of what transpired. Hawkins, or Brasov for that matter, would give a lot to get their hands on what we have... and what we know."

They were slowing, and Tag realized they had finally reached their destination. The garage outside Athens, Georgia, was one that Harden rented under an assumed name. They concealed the Cobra inside, set the locks and alarms, and then walked several blocks to an assuming brick bungalow. Harden deactivated the security system and opened several more locks before allowing them inside.

The furnishings were unremarkable. Harden immediately went to a section of the wall, next to the kitchen and dining nook, and pressed three of its corners in a specific pattern. The panel popped open, revealing a concealed fire safe. Harden turned the combination dial this way and that before finally opening the safe.

Tag whistled. The safe contained three Kalashnikov rifles, close to a dozen thirty-round magazines, a few seventy-five round drum magazines, and cases of 7.62 x 39 caliber Russian surplus ammo. There were various handguns in 9mm and .45 ACP, spare magazines and ammunition for those, and a few different swords and tomahawks. There were also piles of money — stacks of bills in various denominations and currencies.

"Wow," was all Tag could say.

"Are you hungry?" said Harden. "We can secure most of our weapons. One handgun each should be enough. I assume we're safe enough to go grocery shopping here in Athens. I've got a late model Mustang smart-car in the garage here."

"What's with you and the Fords?" asked Tag.

"When the Social Democrats were spending the country into oblivion, a little past the turn of the twenty-first century," said Harden, "the Ford company refused to take public money. I respected that. I've been buying Fords ever since."

"But that was..." Tag started to say.

"Yeah," said Harden. "A long time ago."

"Doesn't it ever... doesn't it ever get a bit much? Hundreds of years worth of memories, all piled up in the same person?"

"I guess it does," said Harden. "You see a lot of things come and go. Things that people go their whole human lifetimes and take for granted. Things they think will never change. I can remember when everybody smoked, for example. *Everybody.* You could sit down next to somebody on an airplane, or in a restaurant, and just light up. It isn't just the laws about smoking that have changed. People just stopped doing it."

"If I were a vampire," said Tag, "I think I would take up smoking. I'd use one of those cigarette holders. It wouldn't hurt me. It would be very stylish."

Harden laughed. "I gave it up myself in the late Aughties."

"The what?"

"Two-thousand nine or so," said Harden. "The taxes they slapped on them made them so damned expensive I resented giving the government all that money."

"Harden..." Tag said. "Don't be offended, but... If you hate Brasov so much, if you're so against government control, why are you only just now trying to meet up with the Resistance? You could have worked with Thomas to step up Cousinry donations to Van Gogh and the other Resistance cells. You could have joined them outright, if you'd wanted to. Why did you only agree to do so now? Was it just Thomas' death?"

"The vampire's conceit," said Harden. "Thomas choosing to die was part of it. Before that, I told myself that if I was patient, if we just worked behind the scenes, things would change slowly. Vampires always believe there's more time. We have *eternity*, after all. But just like mortal men and women, we eventually... end. And there's never enough time to get done what we need to do."

"I can't imagine the life you've led," said Tag. "The people you've known and lost."

"You mentioned Van Gogh," said Harden. "I once met the man he was named for. The painter. I encountered him a few years before his death."

"That's incredible!"

"Not really," said Harden. "I never really cared for his work."

Harden went to the small bar against one wall. "Would you like something to drink? I have some excellent small-batch bourbon. The distillery doesn't exist anymore."

"I'm not much for bourbon," she said. She pointed to a shelf next to the bar. "Is that a shortwave?"

"Yes," said Harden. "It's not exactly state of the art."

"It's huge," said Tag, holding the palm-sized plastic square. Touching the controls, she found it tuned to Conservative Exile. Conservative talk radio and privately owned television networks had been banned by Brasov years before. A number of the contributors to Conservative Exile, even though they used pseudonyms and voice changers, had been found out and murdered since the ban.

"The chair is against the wall," said the modulated voice from the shortwave, "and that means it's time for our Resistance communiqués. Delta seven, forty-one. Charlie eight, sixty-six. Go long, young men. Daphne has removed her veil." Tag switched off the shortwave.

"I remember when the BBC used to broadcast messages like that during the Second World War," said Harden.

"'The chair is against the wall,'" said Tag. "Why is that familiar?"

Harden chuckled. "It's from a movie. Somebody's idea of an ironic joke." He locked eyes with her. "So you'll take me to see Van Gogh?"

"If you'll let me drive the Cobra for just a little."

"I promise," said Harden. "But we'll have to take the smart-car, not the Cobra. Hawkins' people will be looking for the Shelby, so it will have to stay hidden." When she looked disappointed, he said, "Don't worry. The new Mustang is souped-up."

"It's *what*?"

"Bigger engine," said Harden. "Beefed-up suspension. It *hauls*, as the kids say."

"None of the kids say that," said Tag.

"Well, they did a hundred years ago."

Tag went to the refrigerator in the kitchen nook. "You can show me tomorrow. Right now, I need food. I don't suppose you have anything in here that isn't blood," she said. She opened the refrigerator and immediately regretted it. The smell was awful."

"The chocolate milk's gone bad," said Harden. "I haven't stopped here in a while. We'll get more."

"You... drink chocolate milk?" asked Tag, closing the refrigerator and wrinkling her nose.

"Love the stuff. I'm addicted to it."

"But you're a vampire."

"Most of us still enjoy eating ordinary food," said Harden. "Not to mention drinking something other than blood. I could really go for a drink. What do you fancy?"

"How about a bottle of wine?" said Tag. "Maybe... maybe a *jug* of wine."

"That," said Harden, "can be arranged."

Chapter Eight

Near the North Carolina Border

Elizabeth Hawkins sunk her fangs deep into the young man's throat. He struggled as she drained him; she liked it when they struggled. The irony was not lost on her that she felt such disdain for fleshers while feeding regularly on human blood herself. Some needs simply could not be met through... alternative means. She and her people, all of her top men and women, regularly indulged, but it would not do to have the rank and file among her supporters know the truth. She must appear to hold the moral high ground, especially where those prigs in the Cousinry were concerned. Granted, any vampire could smell it if he or she were close enough. But people believed what they wanted to believe. If the centuries she had lived had taught her anything, they had taught her that.

She wore a tube top and the tightest of leather miniskirts. Her stiletto heels were the longest she owned. Here, in the lee of the dumpster behind the road house, the rock music from within was still loud enough to make her breast-bone vibrate. She reveled in the sensations, in the smell of the night air, in the thrill of having brought this man from the bar to the back of the building. Men were so easily seduced.

Her feedings were not usually so colorful. She had needed the escape, had needed the feel of the hunt, to distract her from this latest failure. Simply having a bound man or woman brought to her discreetly by her people would not do. She needed to feel the thrill of the chase and the rush of taking life.

This hunt had been an unexpected treat. She had lured him to the back of the road house, or so she thought, with the implied promise of her half-naked body. No sooner had they reached the dumpster than the wire garrote appeared in his hands. He was some sort of predator, a serial rapist or murderer. He'd thought Elizabeth Hawkins was his next victim.

The idea made her laugh. Bubbles of blood formed at the corner of her mouth. She laughed harder and drank more deeply. The man's struggles grew weaker. The delicious feeling of it almost distracted her from her disappointment over the raid on Thomas Simpson's estate.

Her plan had been to pry the secrets of the Cousinry from Simpson himself. Even in the twilight "death" of a vampire choosing to abstain from feeding, he could have been revived. That bastard Harden had stopped her from doing so — had prevented her from gaining access to the vast fortune the Cousinry had been amassing and nurturing for so many centuries. But her fight against the Cousinry was more than a battle to gain control over those hoarded vampire riches. She wanted to *beat* them, wanted to teach them that their vision of vampires and humans as somehow *equal* was what had to change.

The lion had lain with the lamb long enough.

If Hawkins' faction was to reign supreme, they needed more than the will to dominate humankind. They needed resources, which made the Cousinry's hoard increasingly vital to her plans.

That was, of course, the reason behind her alliance with Brasov. Brasov already held the West in his grasp. He had the infrastructure, the political power, and the wisdom to manage those complex, frequently opposed forces. He kept his various factions warring among themselves, encouraging the Muslim sects to increase their territories while the Fedvamps looked the other way. It was a brilliant strategy; even the Resistance spent a disproportionate amount of time locked in largely pointless combat with the Basij. All the while Brasov, maintained his grip on power.

Hawkins' victim finally stopped moving. She felt his pulse stop, felt the luscious, rhythmic pump of blood go still. Disgusted, she rolled the body off her lap and stood. She used the back of her hand to wipe blood from her face.

Brasov. Vlad Tepes. By whatever name, he roused her passion still. Her failure to maintain their alliance bothered her every day. But she would not be controlled, and Brasov was nothing if not a control freak. He could not have a loose cannon, some mere *woman* who would not follow his orders to the letter, interfering in his carefully laid plans. And so he had sought to murder her. What had it been... twenty years now? It felt like yesterday. For all his many exceptional qualities, Brasov had little but contempt for women. He had never been able to see Hawkins as his equal. It was why she had defied him... and why their alliance had been doomed from the start.

The position in which that left her was... difficult, and growing more so. Her people followed her because they believed in her — and in her vision of vampire supremacy. Brasov offered that supremacy, but at the price of swearing fealty to him and his whims. Hawkins offered the same... but her own whims were considerably more pleasant and more immediate than Brasov's long-term machinations. It was difficult for a vampire to look at Brasov's complex plans and see the benefits to that vampire of Vlad's goals. She grasped that. She also knew that, unchecked, Brasov would have dominion over the modern world. It was why she had sought him out in the first place.

Without the troops, control infrastructure, and wealth that Brasov controlled, Hawkins had to find that strength elsewhere. The threat to her following was more immediate than their lack of a means to put her visions in place at the national level. If Brasov were not eliminated, he would walk over everything and everyone who opposed him. His assassination attempts on her had grown infrequent over the last two decades, but when it became clear to him that Hawkins was working actively to unseat him, that she was as great a threat to him as the Resistance, he would take it personally. That was Vlad's nature. He was adept at prioritizing, placing immediate threats and goals in perspective against long-term ones... but he forgot nothing, ever.

The wild, indomitable spirit that was Hawkins' own nature was the reason Vlad had betrayed her. He would not tolerate anyone in his circle he could not control. She had left the Cousinry because their methods were too limited, their views unrealistic. So where did that leave her? Her following was loyal... but they were no match, by themselves for Brasov's might.

Years of planning had been ruined by Vincent Harden. But Harden, even as he vexed her, could yet be the tool she needed. Simpson would not have let the secrets of the Cousinry die with him. Harden had been there at the end; Harden was, in every way that mattered, Simpson's adopted son. He would have the information she required.

Almost reluctantly, she stood. The warm glow that suffused her body when she fed still lingered. The Cadillac smart-car, with Caspian behind the wheel, was waiting for her at the rear of the road house parking lot. She slipped into the back.

"Take me home, Caspian," she said. She added, "Any word since this morning on Brasov's strange troop movements?"

"Only the same report," said Caspian. "Now repeated by several of our spies within Brasov's organization. He is hiding something. Something big. A weapon, perhaps. Something requiring heavy security. Many men and much equipment has been diverted in the last two weeks for this purpose."

"Send word through our network," she told him, sinking back into her seat. "Tell them to work harder. Find out what it is. Find out *where* it is. If Brasov has a secret weapon, we need to find it before he can use it."

"As you instruct."

"Put our people on patrol for Harden, too," said Hawkins, as Caspian pulled out of the parking lot. "He's no doubt gone to ground somewhere, but perhaps we'll get lucky. Find someone who can tell me about this girl who was with him, too. She looked familiar to me. Ask Arturo when he recovers." She paused. "He *is* recovering?"

"Slowly," said Caspian. "I'm having him seen to. Harden very nearly severed his head from his neck. He was lucky to escape."

The motion of the car was lulling Hawkins to sleep. "If he cannot be of use to us," she said dreamily, "his luck will have run out."

* * *

Harden fired his musket. The redcoat soldier went down. They were far from the skirmish lines; the enemy patrol had been separated from the main force of loyalists, making for easy pickings for Harden and the men shoring up Washington's left flank. Harden dropped his musket, drew his pistols, and fired those in rapid succession. Two more redcoats joined the dead. The last man, an officer, held a saber.

His hand went to the hunting sword at his waist. He drew the weapon and charged the enemy. His steps, on the broken terrain of the creek bed, were uncertain, clumsy.

Harden felt the saber glance off his ribs, felt warm blood soak his flank. His hunting sword found its mark, up and under the British soldier's chin. The man's eyes went wide. Harden's nostrils flared as the smell of the man's blood hit him full in the face.

The lust he felt, the urge to feed, hit him harder than ever. He bared his fangs before he could help himself.

Just this once. He's already dying. It would be so easy—

* * *

"Harden," said Tag, crouching next the edge of the couch. "Are you all right?"

Harden turned, apparently realizing where he was. He had fallen asleep on the sofa in the rented bungalow.

"Sorry," he said. "It was an exhausting day." He sat up and rubbed at his eyes. "Why did you ask me if I was all right?"

"You were shouting in your sleep," said Tag. She went back to the kitchen nook, where she had been cooking. She resumed stirring the pot of canned tomato sauce she was heating.

"What did I say?"

"Nothing intelligible," said Tag. "Just... noises. Growling, almost."

Harden said nothing to that. He started to stand, to stretch, when his phone began to vibrate on the coffee table. He had left it plugged into its remote charger. He put the piece of glass to his ear. "Yes," he said.

Who would be calling him? One of the Cousinry? An ally she didn't know about? Tag had no idea. Nothing about the timing was necessarily suspicious, but anything was possible with Elizabeth Hawkins gunning for them.

"Marly!" said Harden. "I should warn you. My battery is very low."

That was a code if ever Tag had heard one. In hushed tones, Harden conferred with whomever this "Marly" might be. She couldn't make out most of it, nor did she want to seem to be eavesdropping. She was still very curious.

"I love you," Harden finally said. "Yes. Okay. Remember what I've said. I'll contact you as soon as it's safe." He put the phone back on the table and noticed her staring at him. "What?"

"Nothing," said Tag. "I just didn't... Well, I didn't realize you had a woman somewhere. I guess it makes sense that you would. It's just..." Dammit! She could feel her face growing red. She hated to admit that Harden was extremely handsome and that fact was not lost on her. He might be hundreds of years old, but he looked 30, and there was something about his eyes—

Harden was laughing. She started to open her mouth to tell him off, anger and humiliation welling up within her, when he held up a hand.

"No," said Harden. "Nothing like that. Marlena is my *daughter*."

She almost dropped the wooden spoon into the spaghetti sauce. "But vampires can't have children."

"No," said Harden, sounding suddenly wistful. "They can't." His tone changed, becoming uglier. "All vampires are made, never born," he said. "Remember?"

It was an often-repeated slogan, the kind of thing people said when they wanted to remind themselves that vampires were not a people, not a species, but a communicable disease.

"I'm sorry," she said. "I didn't mean—"

"No," he said, holding up his hand again. "*I'm* sorry. It's been too long since I spent time with anyone who wasn't Thomas... and far too long since I shared dinner with a beautiful woman. Forgive my terrible manners, please. The food smells delicious."

She felt herself blushing again, this time for all the right reasons.

* * *

The jug of wine sat on the table between them. Harden had cleared the dinner plates away. The tabletop candles flickered as they sat, enjoying some classical music from the antique laser player in the cabinet in the living room. Tag had marveled at the machine when she saw it. No one had them anymore. They were as obsolete, Harden reflected, as Harden himself sometimes felt.

"I'm a man of simple tastes, really," he said, sipping from his wine glass. Tag sat across from him, her hands folded around her own glass, watching him. "I like simple, efficient things that work well. I like to plan ahead. I like to be smarter than the enemies I'll face."

"But the infomercial," said Tag. "The one that outed the vampires once and for all. You're all supposed to be sleeping under gilded capes and guarding vast hoarded fortunes, like a bunch of... what was the term they used in the recording? 'Liver-chotskies.'"

Harden nearly snorted his wine. "Liberace," he said. "Like a bunch of Liberaces."

"Why is that funny?" asked Tag. "Is that a vampire thing?"

"No," said Harden, struggling not to laugh. "Liberace wasn't a vampire thing. He wasn't a *thing* at all. He was a man. A mortal man, as far as I know. He was piano player known for his flamboyant style."

"Oh," said Tag. "You hear so many things about that video."

"It wasn't completely accurate," Harden told her, sipping more of his wine. His nasal sinuses burned. "Most vampires lie as I do. We enjoy eating 'normal' food, but we need blood as part of our diet. We take that blood from domestic animals, like cows, sheep, and pigs. The Cousinry is an ancient fraternal order of vampires, once the ruling body that governed most of our kind. We kept knowledge of vampires secret for hundreds of years. One of our most stringent laws is the requirement not to feed from humans."

"But Hawkins and her people have no such rule."

"Hawkins' following is made up of fanatics," said Harden, darkening. "She split from the Cousinry centuries ago because she, and those who follow her, believe humans should be subservient to vampires — that vampires should form a ruling elite, an undead aristocracy. Someone like Hawkins feeds from humans both because it's... pleasurable... and because it's a reminder that humans are, in her eyes, cattle. Her people won't touch human food — only human beings themselves. We call vampires who do that 'fleshers.'"

"I've never heard that term."

"It's something we use amongst ourselves," Harden admitted. "Most fleshers believe a diet consisting only of human blood makes them stronger and faster. It might be something in the blood, or it might be the savagery required to feed exclusively on people. Depends on who you ask. The Cousinry, through the ages, has tried to determine scientifically if that's so. There's no proof of it."

"The media say vampires feeding off humans is a myth," said Tag. "Something spread to foment anti-vampire hatred."

"Propaganda," said Harden. "Probably the work of Brasov himself, who's rumored to feed on human beings daily."

"So nobody knows for sure," said Tag.

"I know," said Harden. "I've fed on human blood."

Tag recoiled. "You *have*?"

"Marlena," said Harden. "She... volunteered her own blood to me. I was weak. I needed strength to save her and her mother from Hawkins. But I had never fed from donor human beings before; I didn't know how much to safely take. If I hadn't turned Marlena to save her life, she would have died."

Tag thought about that for a moment. She leaned forward again, perhaps sensing that Harden wanted to talk. He needed to, really; Thomas Simpson's death, his dream, the call from Marlena... they had all put him in a thoughtful mood. He needed to get his head straight.

"How old is Hawkins?" she asked.

"Nobody really knows," said Harden. "Much older than me, at the very least. It's been said that she was sixteen when she was turned. That she might well have been a mistress to the Roman emperor, Caligula, and later to Nero. She hates Christians and is said by some vampires within Church hierarchy to have aided Nero in his persecution of the faith."

"There are vampires in the Church?"

"What's left of it," said Harden. "Vatican City can't hold out forever. But yes, there are vampires within its ranks. Most human organizations have at least a few highly placed undead members. It was part of Thomas' vision. He thought vampires, with their centuries of experience, could help guide humani-

71

ty. That we could help each other down through the years to create a better world. He once told me that he saw me as the kind of vampire we should strive to become, rather than what vampires have devolved to be since Hawkins and her people outed us to the world."

"That was Hawkins? Some people say Brasov was in on it."

"He may have been," said Harden. There was hate in his voice now. "Throughout modern history," he added quietly, "whenever you find something horrible has happened, you will find Elizabeth Hawkins or Woodrow Brasov right in the middle of it."

Chapter Nine

Washington, District of Brasovia

"In 1461," said Woodrow Brasov, his index finger on the "record" icon of his phone's screen, "a Turk named Altan bin Ramseur was dragged from the column of prisoners held by Vlad Tepes. That Turk was a Captain in the army of Sultan Mehmed II. He was one of thousands of Turkish prisoners tormented by the forces of Dracula, also known," Brasov paused for effect, "as Vlad the Impaler."

"On the day in question," Brasov continued, "many hundreds of Turks have already been executed. Dracula's army is retreating after a disastrous attempt to murder the Sultan. They are employing a scorched-Earth policy in conjunction with the usual mutilations, murders, and impalements. Altan bin Ramseur was a professional soldier, as was his father, as was his father's father. Despite many wounds and the malnutrition he has incurred in his captivity, he is determined to die in battle. He has heard the stories of Dracula, of the Son of the Devil. He will take the monster, Dracula, to hell with him. Snatching a sword, he hacks his way through the slave-master and more than a half dozen of Dracula's private guard. He fights Vlad Tepes... and he wins, scoring a deadly blow on Vlad Tepes. But though the monster staggers and falls, he rises again, undead. If not for the blood on his armor, Altan bin Ramseur would think his blade had missed."

Brasov took his finger from the phone and cleared his throat. He pressed the icon once more and continued. "God," he said, "truly is great, but Allah's will is not with Altan bin Ramseur this day. The monster Dracula, insane with rage, orders his men from the scene. He throttles bin Ramseur, promising the Turk Captain that he will suffer as no man has suffered. Dracula, a vampire, will give Altan bin Ramseur the terrible curse of eternal life... only so the Turk may know what it is to live impaled on a pike, rising and dying with each passing day. These will truly be the tortures of the damned, for bin Ramseur, craving human blood, will feel hours to days and then to weeks of agony. Only with total starvation will the undead bin Ramseur's vampiric life finally expire. And by then, he will be quite insane... or so Vlad Tepes believes."

Brasov released the phone and swiped the screen with his thumb. The recording would be filed in his encrypted etherway. There would be many more recordings, many more memoirs to commit to memory. Woodrow Brasov intended to tell the entire world his history... once that world was finally, firmly under his grasp.

Only then would the human and vampire worlds know the truth. To human beings, Woodrow Brasov was the first openly vampire politician to hold high elected office. To other vampires, Brasov was rumored to be Vlad Tepes, Voivode of Wallachia. Neither world knew the truth: That he, Woodrow Brasov, was Altan bin Ramseur.

It had taken him a very long time to rejoin his people after freeing himself from the pike on which Dracula impaled him. It had taken still longer to raise the necessary forces. Altan bin Ramseur was then a vampire; he enlisted the help of Turkish troops loyal to him, creating a platoon of Janissaries to aid him on his quest. The battle with Vlad Tepes, the hunt for Dracula and for Altan bin Ramseur's revenge, had taken more than four hundred and fifty years. By the time he finally defeated Vlad Tepes, killing him and taking his identity, he had been planning the switch for decades.

Vampire kind did not know the name of Altan bin Ramseur... but it knew Vlad Tepes. To Vlad Tepes' banner would other vampires flock, if only Vlad III finally gave them something to follow. For all his ferocity in battle, the Prince of Wallachia was a poor strategist. It was why he had lost his throne to Prince Basarab in 1477. History recorded his death at the hands of disloyal Wallachian boyars who were presumably also fighting the Turks. The truth was that Vlad Tepes, knowing his third reign was unsustainable, had faked his death and moved on. That cunning did not save him when bin Ramseur and his Janissaries finally ran the man to ground.

With Dracula dead, bin Ramseur had taken his name. No one knew the many lifetimes of Vlad Tepes better than Altan bin Ramseur. In his hatred, in his thirst for revenge, bin Ramseur had learned everything about his enemy. He had searched out every piece of lore, every fact, every written account. He had interviewed those who claimed to have witnessed Dracula's early life. He had interrogated other vampires believed to have knowledge of his foe. But in plumbing the depths of Vlad Tepes' secrets, he had learned something much, much more important. By the time he finally separated Dracula's head from his neck, granting his hated enemy a much cleaner death than ever Vlad III had given another, bin Ramseur was already moving on to bigger and better plans.

His plan hinged on his unquestioned hold over the American political machine... and his influence among the Muslim communities even now eating away what was once America. To this day, he regretted the Muslims he had been forced to order killed by his Janissaries in the plot to alienate the Cousinry... but they were now in the arms of Allah. Their deaths had served him well. The Christians, the Jews, and all other infidels would die; the Cousinry would be destroyed; Elizabeth Hawkins and her cult of personality would be put to the swords. Altan bin Ramseur, as Brasov, would usher in a new, golden age, a worldwide vampire caliphate that would be consolidated under his iron fist.

Many steps in his plan remained. One critical maneuver was the culmination of years of subtle manipulation on his part. Hawkins was slow to come to it, but come to it she would: she must, if she wished to survive, ally herself once more with the Cousinry and thus the Resistance. With Hawkins' corrosive influence among their ranks, the Resistance would not be able to field a unified front against him. Their attacks would be successful enough to lull them into a false sense of hope. Then bin Ramseur's Fedvamps would eliminate them, finally crushing all vampire opposition in the North America.

Meanwhile, bin Ramseur's Janissaries were positioning themselves to provoke the cartels now flooding the American states along the nation's porous border with Mexico. Strategic attacks on cartel leadership would enrage the cartels, increasing the tensions on the southern border to the breaking point. The National Guard, the Reserve, and the regular forces of the United States military would be deployed to fight along the border, drawing resources from the many fronts around the world where American military forces still fought doomed battles with the world's Islamist factions.

Right now, those forces were stretched to the breaking point. Brasov had been slowing the flow of funds, troops, and equipment to the world's Islamist hot zones for some time. Drawing further resources to the southern border would finally snap the will of the American military. Denied resupply, faltering and demoralized, the Americans would be forced to admit defeat in the battle with Islam. But America's military would never come home. Altan bin Ramseur would see to it that the American Navy was redeployed to the coasts of North America, as his vampire shock troops, strategically placed at all levels of the American military, seized control.

Once global Islamic domination was assured, bin Ramseur would declare full Sharia Law throughout North American. He would reveal himself, finally, as Altan bin Ramseur. He would release his biography to the world. He would declare himself Caliph of the "vampire nation" — a term that was already falling into common use. It had originally referred to non-aligned vampires, those not affiliated with the Cousinry. They were supposed to be the "silent majority" of the undead. Now, however, the vampire nation was the sum total of world vampires. It was all of them. As different as the undead could be, it had been impossible to consolidate them under one political aegis in years past. Now, with Brasov's star on the rise and his power growing, it would finally become a possibility. And that possibility was about to become a reality. His conquest would finally be complete.

The intercom on his desk in the Oval Office buzzed. Without announcement, the door to the office opened, admitting Orin Weld. The gaunt, awkward Weld was a human vampire-worshipper, convinced that one day Woodrow Brasov would reward him by turning him. He was an ill-kempt specimen of human kind, wan and nervous at the best of times, but he possessed an extraordinarily organized mind... and he was utterly loyal to Brasov. Once, the scarecrow of a man had taken a stake in the shoulder, the weapon of a would-be assassin who attempted to murder Brasov at a rally in California. As Brasov stood over the wounded man, his Fedvamp bodyguards ripping the assassin to pieces (but discreetly and off camera), Weld had reached out to Brasov... holding a bloodied, crumpled resume in his hand.

Weld had long worshipped Brasov. He was one of many devoted human fans who saw a vampire president as the hope for America's future. Brasov knew zealotry when he saw it. He had quickly given Weld the position the man so earnestly desired. Since that time, Weld had not only served Brasov well; he served as a constant reminder of the Brasov Administration's devotion to camaraderie and coexistence with humankind. So the American state-controlled media dutifully reported.

"What is it, Orin?" said Brasov.

"President Montenegro-Ibanez is waiting for you in the anteroom, sir," said Orin, practically bowing in Brasov's presence.

Brasov nodded. He had forgotten his meeting with the Mexican president. Jose Montenegro-Ibanez presided over the first Mexico in decades to run free of apparent corruption. This was thanks to the efforts of Brasov's vampires, who had insinuated themselves — with Mexico's tacit cooperation — into every level of the Mexican government.

"And my dinner?" said Brasov.

"Waiting for you in the Lincoln Bedroom, sir," said Weld. "She is quite lovely."

"Thank you," said Brasov. At this, Weld beamed with joy. It took only the slightest approval or recognition from his undead god-emperor, as the vampire cults saw Brasov, to make Weld practically giddy.

"Sir, I apologize, but if I may... the kitchen has a question," said Weld, scraping before Brasov. "I've told them time and again that only women will do, but they say they've obtained several young men who seem quite healthy, and they enquire as to whether you would find them an acceptable repast." Weld cringed as if he feared he might be struck. "I told them yet again that this would not be palatable to you, sir."

"Your instincts are correct," said Brasov simply. "Inform the kitchen that I dine only on women, and if there is some misunderstanding to that effect, I will be happy to speak with them directly and explain it to them. I will see the President Montenegro-Ibanez now."

"Yes, sir," said Weld. He excused himself, bowing low.

Altan bin Ramseur had fed on men before, of course, but only in the heat of battle, or as a final means of vanquishing an enemy. For a male to feed on other males simply for sustenance was... unmanly.

Weld reappeared in the doors to the Oval Office. "President Jose Montenegro-Ibanez," he announced.

"Thank you, Orin," said Brasov, grinning widely. "That will be all for this evening. Except... Have Ibn al Farir summoned. I have need of him."

Weld actually shuddered. "Of course, sir," he said. "Thank you, President Brasov, sir." He closed the doors quietly between them.

"Please, Jose," said Brasov. He indicated the chairs before the Resolute Desk.

President Jose Montenegro-Ibanez rose to the Presidency after the "tragic death" of his predecessor, President Carlos Villanueva, who was killed in an explosion caused by "unknown assassins." In point of fact, the killers were Fedvamps in the employ of Brasov. That had been the start of a very long and profitable relationship between the two men. Brasov regularly supplied Montenegro-Ibanez with payments of gold, human women who were part of the North American sex-trafficking trade, weapons, training for the Mexican secret police, and of legions of Fedvamps on loan from Brasov's administration. In return, Brasov received Montenegro-Ibanez' complete cooperation in his long-term plans. The Mexican president actually believed his nation would be exempt from North American Sharia when Brasov implemented it. Well. There was no accounting for naiveté.

"The reconquista is ready to commence," Montenegro-Ibanez reported. "My Cartel troops on the border, together with your Fedvamps, require only your signal to proceed."

"I need you to delay the attack," Brasov said. "The Texans are too heavily armed at this time for your Cartels to succeed against them. I need time to send you more Fedvamps if the operation is to succeed."

"This delay is... unwelcome."

"To me as well," said Brasov. "But I need to time to consolidate support in the neighboring states if I am to subdue Texas and Georgia. I also need time to move more human military troops out of the country before we make our move. Within a few weeks, the last of the remaining full-readiness units will ship out. By the time their commanders realize the country has been seized by my Fedvamp forces, backed by Islamist troops from the Sharia enclaves, I will have cut supply lines overseas and choked off military funding within the government here. Any remaining human resistance can be eliminated by my vampire soldiers. Already, the vast majority of human military troops are engaged overseas. My Fedvamps grow in number almost exponentially. Time is our friend, Jose."

"You will keep your word?" said Montenegro-Ibanez.

"Arizona, New Mexico, and southern California will return to Mexican control," said Brasov easily.

Montenegro-Ibanez stood. "Then we will wait for your signal," he said, nodding. "You must hate your country very much, amigo."

"On the contrary, Jose," said Brasov. "I *love* America. I love the promise of what America can be. Our nation simply needs the right guidance. Under my rule, it will receive that. Under my rule, a consolidated North America will finally become one nation under Allah."

* * *

The torture Adam now endured was not the worst he had experienced.

In the millennia of his existence he had been subjected to much greater pain. As he sat chained to the wooden chair in the darkened chamber, the monitor on the wall began to brighten. Only a vampire, with a vampire's command of the visible spectrum, would be able to perceive the change in illumination that preceeded the display switching on. Adam could see it. The display was his only companion in this dark place.

His thirst was great. He had consumed nothing since being secured within the chamber three weeks past.

The chair was wired for electricity. At irregular intervals, electrodes secured to his genitals delivered a shock through his body.

The air was thick with caustic chemicals, pumped in through ventilation ducts set within the floor. His eyes watered whenever he opened them. With every breath, his lungs burned, scorching his throat.

No, it was not the worst prison he had endured. Not by a very great margin.

The screen was on. The face of the man called Woodrow Brasov peered at him. Now Brasov would say the thing he always said.

"Tell me what I want to know," Brasov's voice said from speakers set within the concrete walls.

"I can't tell you," Adam said. "I can't tell you because I don't remember."

"There are many vampires in the world who are not allied with my forces," said Brasov. "Vampires who know nothing of the Cousinry. Vampires who have never heard of Elizabeth Hawkins. Can you tell me where they are? Can you tell me their numbers?"

"How many vampires people the world?" said Adam. He swallowed, hard. His throat was raw. "I don't know. I can't say."

"Tell me of your birth," said Brasov. "Tell me how you came to be a vampire."

"I can't tell you," Adam repeated. "I can't tell you because I don't remember."

"You leave me no choice," said Brasov. "I have no recourse but to send to you Ibn al Farir. Do you know that name?"

"A butcher," said Adam. "A murderer. A mad dog."

"He is all those things," said Brasov. "And more. You will suffer as no creature has when you are at his mercy."

"You will make him ask me the same questions," said Adam.

"Yes," said Brasov. "Tell me what I want to know, Adam. Tell me the secret of your birth and I will release you."

"You will never release me, Woodrow Brasov," said Adam. "We both know this."

"And why is that?" asked Brasov.

"Because," said Adam. "I know that you are not, and never were, Vlad Tepes."

Chapter Ten

Blue Ridge Mountains, Northern Georgia

The mirror on the passenger side of the Mustang exploded.

"Hold on!" Harden said. He put his foot to the floor. The Mustang's custom engine growled, causing "economy" warning lights to blink on the dash. The Mustang was a hybrid, using both electric power and flexfuel. Harden reached out and hit a switch wired to the underside of the dash. The warning lights winked out.

Tag wrestled her Thompson into position between her knees and rolled down her window. Harden had explained the smart-car override to her. If they encountered any Fedvamps, or Hawkins' people had Fedvamp tech at their disposal, they could send a signal to shut down the smart-car circuits and switch off the vehicle. It was illegal to circumvent a smart-car's automatic intervention circuitry, but then, neither one of them was exactly a stickler for following the law.

Their trip into the mountains that morning had been peaceful enough... until the Mustang had driven past a pair of black Hybrid SUVs parked at an overlook pull-off. New SUVs were restricted to only certain purchasers: Governments, Sharia enclaves, law enforcement, and anyone who could get a carbon credit voucher. The vouchers were traded on the black market. These SUVs were jet black, with spotlights and massive brush-guard bumpers. The lack of insignia made them Hawkins' people. Harden had poured on the speed after passing them. Enough time passed that Tag thought maybe they'd been missed, that they hadn't been made.

Then the gunfire had started.

"She's put our descriptions out to her people," said Harden, his knuckles white on the Mustang's wheel. "They're not looking for the car. They're looking for *us*."

Tag cocked the Thompson and leaned out her window. She triggered a long burst of .45 auto, making the front bumper of the lead SUV spark and chime. Bullet holes starred the windshield and struck the passenger and driver. The driver appeared not to notice; the passenger hit the dash in a bloody heap.

"Vampires and humans," said Tag, ducking back into the vehicle. The Mustang began to shake. Bullets shattered the rear windshield and Tag yelled in alarm, ducking down lower in her seat. Something struck the driver's side rear tire.

"Run-flats," said Harden. "But they won't last forever. I can't outrun them," said Harden. "Not on these mountain roads, not with all their low-end torque. I need straightaway. We're going to have to do something else before they put too many holes in us."

Tag fired off another burst. She turned back to Harden. "Do what?"

"Plan B," said Harden. "Switch with me."

"Do *what*?"

"Take the wheel!" Harden yelled. He revved the motor, giving them a burst of speed. The curve coming up was very tight. *Steep Drop Off*, read one sign. *Reduce Speed Ahead*.

"Harden!" shouted Tag. She complied nonetheless, sliding awkwardly under him as he rolled over her. Once in his seat, she got her foot on the brake, then the gas, fish-tailing the Mustang around the deadly curve. Somehow, she kept them from sliding down the side of the mountain.

"I told you I'd let you drive," shot Harden. He unlimbered the tomahawk he had put on his belt that morning. He also drew a .45 automatic, one of the Commander-length pistols he carried in his shoulder rig. "Slow down a little. Let the lead truck get up close behind us.

"What are you about to do?" Tag asked.

"Something very stupid," he said, and climbed out the passenger-side window.

Tag nearly lost control when she saw him continue to climb. Hanging from the passenger-side roof-line with his feet wedged under him, he coiled and... *leapt*, jumping from the Mustang to the hood of the pursuing SUV.

Muzzle flashes strobed as Harden emptied his .45 into the windshield of the truck. Then he was smashing out the remaining pebbles of safety glass with his tomahawk, cleaving a hole large enough to admit him. The driver was shooting, pumping bullets into Harden's chest, but they did nothing to stop him. The Cousinry vampire tucked his pistol in his waistband and shouldered his way through the hole he'd made, practically landing in the driver's lap.

The vampire tried to plunge his fangs into Harden's neck, but Harden was faster. He cleaved the driver's skull with his tomahawk, driving the blade deep, nearly splitting the vampire's head in two. The vampire screamed in agony. Harden opened the door and the SUV's driver fell from the vehicle, tumbling until he was run over by the second SUV. He was screaming and cursing the entire time.

That was the thing about vampires. You could split their skulls, but that wasn't enough to kill them.

The second SUV pulled up alongside. As the Mustang and then the two SUVs roared past a dirt fire road, a third SUV joined the chase.

Great, thought Harden, rolling his eyes. *Reinforcements.*

Automatic gunfire from the second SUV started ripping through the truck. The bullets in Harden's chest were already pushing their way out of his body, expelled as his body healed itself. He felt the bloody wound being ripped through his thigh; a Kalashnikov bullet punched through the other side of the truck. Harden reached out, grabbed the A-frame of the driver-side door, and wrenched the door from the hinges. He let it go and watched it crash into the windshield of the third truck, shattering it.

A quick jerk of the wheel and a hard boot to the accelerator were all he needed to shove the second truck off the road. He timed it just right, waiting for the next hairpin mountain turn. Then he used the weight of the truck to shove the second SUV through the guardrail. He didn't bother to watch it crash along the rocks below.

Now it was Harden's turn to slow down. He slammed on the brakes and, when the third SUV drew abreast, he flung himself through his open doorway. Ripping the third truck's passenger-side door away, he dove inside the truck's cabin.

The shotgun-seat gunner was human. Harden snapped his neck easily, tossing the body out the opening behind him. The vampire behind the wheel went for his own holstered gun, but it was in flap holster on his belt. It might as well have been back at home in a gun safe. Harden drew his second Commander .45, rammed the barrel toward the vampire's eyes, and pulled the trigger as fast as he could.

The muzzle blast liquefied the vampire's eyes and scorched the bridge of his nose. He shrieked in pain.

Harden reached down and wrenched the steering column loose.

The truck spun out of control. Harden had just enough time to throw himself back out the gaping passenger side before the third vehicle, too, plunged through the flimsy guardrail and down the side of the mountain. The momentum of his fall caused Harden to bounce, crash, and roll, skidding to a stop on the asphalt, bleeding from several massive abrasions.

He looked up and saw white reverse-lights. Tag was backing the Mustang toward him. The rear tires had been shot, but they would run long enough to get them to cover so he could use the chemical flat-foam in the trunk. The Ford was pocked with bullet holes and missing its rear window, but it was still functional. They had survived the encounter.

Tag pulled up next to him. Her eyes walked up and down him, her expression horrified. "Are you all right?"

Harden pointed.

Vampires were climbing up over the edge of the curve, having made their way from the wrecks below. Harden climbed into the Ford and Tag put the accelerator against the firewall. The powerful Mustang burned out, leaving a trail of smoke, as they sped into the next curve.

"Careful," Hardened warned. "You'll have us up on two wheels."

Tag, however, was watching the rearview mirror. The surviving vampires were chasing them on *foot*, running at least 80 kilometers per hour. A few more gunshots rang out, but the vampire were no match for Harden's supercharged Mustang. Gradually, their pursuers disappeared from the rearview.

"They'll have called in our location," said Harden. "We've got to get off the main road, if we can."

"I know some back trails," said Tag. "We'll get to Van Gogh. But we're going to need to find somewhere to camp for the night."

Harden looked down at his shredded clothes. His wounds were already healed.

"I wouldn't mind a chance to rest and change clothes," he said.

Tag shook her head at the thought of how much damage he had just shrugged off. "Like I said," she laughed. "Stubborn."

* * *

"I was born in Pennsylvania in 1747," said Harden. He was staring into the small campfire they had built, which was itself concealed in a deep fire pit. Tag warmed her hands. The day had been warm, but the night was a cold one. She tried not to shiver. "Thomas was my second father. I was a young officer in George Washington's army at Valley Forge during the winter of 1777 to 1778... and I very nearly died there. I owe my life to another of Washington's officers, a Frenchman named Pierre Lafontaine. He was from the Alsace-Lorraine region, assigned as an aid to Baron Friedrich Wilhelm von Steuben. He had the most amazing accent. Lafontaine was fluent in French and German, and he could manage in English, but I think he was never entirely certain which language he was speaking."

Tag could not help but stare at Harden, who looked particularly handsome in the glow of the fire. "He saved you in battle?" she asked.

"No," said Harden. "Not at all. I contracted typhoid fever."

"Was that bad?"

"About one in three died from it back then," said Harden. Even with anti-biotics, it kills about one in a hundred of its victims." He looked up from the fire. "Are you cold? You look cold. You can come around to this side, if you want."

She did so. Moving closer to Harden for warmth, she almost started. "You're... cold."

"Colder," said Harden, laughing. "Not like ice, or anything. I breath and my blood pumps, but it doesn't carry heat the same way as a human being's."

Harden was still warmer than the outside air. She got as close to him as she dared, pressing against him and enjoying the reflected warmth of the fire. "So how did this Lafontaine save you from Typhoid?"

"I guess you could say I was well-educated for a colonial, and I was detailed to help translate von Steuben's training manuals from French to English. The Baron could speak German and he knew French, but he could not write in English, nor was Lafontaine's English as good as it needed to be. So I helped him, and we produced military training manuals for Washington's troops based on von Steuben's work."

"Typhoid," prompted Tag.

Harden laughed again. "I forget not everybody is as patient as I am," he joked. "I saved Lafontaine's life in April of 1778. It was the Battle of White Marsh, the last major engagement before winter camp at Valley Forge. I guess he never forget that, because when I got sick, Lafontaine got worried. He knew that one of the women among the camp followers, the widow of a dead Sergeant, was a vampire. How he knew about us, how he was privy to the inner workings of the Cousinry back then, I don't know. I'm hopeful Thomas' journal might have details like that. Lafontaine went to the vampires and asked her to turn me, to save me."

"He must have liked you a lot."

"He needed me to translate," said Harden. "My existence was necessary to the training of the men. Lafontaine himself called his motives purely selfish. Thomas was turned in much the same way, you know. It was the Battle of Hastings, in October of 1066. He was just four months past his twentieth birthday. I used to love to tease him about looking younger than me. People would assume he was my son, and I, his youthful-looking father. It drove him crazy."

"So when you were turned you were..."

"Thirty-one," said Harden. "I was just thirty-one years old and at death's door when the vampire woman finally acceded to Lafontaine's request. Her name was Marie Holliday. I owe her a great debt."

"For saving you?"

"For stopping me from slaughtering my fellow soldiers," said Harden. "Marie knew of other vampires in Washington's encampment. We can tell our own. She summoned several of them to hold me down, to keep me subdued during the worst of the birth-thirst that plagues vampires when they are turned. Because of them, I never drank human blood. If not for Marlena, I never would have. And I never will again."

"Your adopted daughter," said Tag.

"Marlena was only sixteen when I was forced to turn her to save her life. She's a fashion model now. With the right makeup and wardrobe, she passes for twenty-one. But I will always regret my hand in making her a vampire. It's why I feel so strongly about feeding from humans. Never again."

Tag nodded. She yawned and then looked horrified. "Oh, Vincent," she said. "I'm sorry. It's not you. I didn't mean—"

Harden chuckled. "No, I understand. It's been a long day. You should get some sleep. My own need for rest is considerably less than yours, so I'm going to go stretch my legs. Do me a favor and don't shoot me when I come back."

"I'll do my best," said Tag. As Harden stood, Tag started laughing quietly."

"What is it?" said Harden.

"It's just that you're a vampire," said Tag, "and you basically just told me you're a night person."

* * *

As morning dawned, Harden returned to the campfire. He had found a white-tailed deer in the woods, caught it easily, and killed it, drinking his fill. The he had butchered it and now carried it back over his shoulders. There would be roast venison on the menu the next time they stopped to make camp—

Something was wrong.

He smelled the presence of human beings, of men and guns, before he was in sight of their little camp. Dropping the deer, he drew his pistols and crept forward, ready to fight. As he got closer, he saw Tag standing near the sputtering fire. A man he had never seen stood talking to her. He cut quite a figure,

87

reminiscent of Che Guevara: olive-drab BDUs, black beret, a checkered red-and-black shemaugh wrapped loosely around his throat. He had a Kalashnikov slung over his shoulder and wore a pair of single-action revolvers tied down low in Cowboy-style leather holsters on his thighs. Bands of ammunition for the pistols crossed his chest at from shoulder to hip.

Harden was capable of complete silence in the woods, but he knew that would not be appreciated here. Tag's body language was carefully neutral, neither comfortable nor suspicious. Choosing his steps carefully, Harden deliberately stepped on a twig and broke it.

Van Gogh's men brought their weapons up, training them on Harden.

"Van," said Tag. "That's him. He's with me."

"Then I gather our weapons will have little effect," said Van Gogh. "Unless we choose to use... other weapons."

At the signal, Van Gogh's men slung their Kalashnikovs and drew machetes from MOLLE-compatible scabbards on their packs. Harden thumbed back the hammers on his .45s.

"Van!" hissed Tag. "He's with *me*."

"We're all friends here," said Harden.

"We are not friends," said Van Gogh. He had a strong Hispanic accent, which Harden's ear thought might be slightly exaggerated for effect. "However, we could someday *become* friends. I am always in the market for friends. But this trust, it is not so quick in all cases, is it? For example, Tag tells me you wish for the Cousinry and the Resistance to work together, not merely to offer your support in the form of money and weapons."

"Yes," said Harden. "Thomas bequeathed control of the Cousinry to me. I intend to honor his memory by bringing the fight to Brasov. I want to bring him down once and for all. Trying to do things slowly and patiently... it isn't working. It isn't enough. I'm ready to join the fight in earnest."

"This is welcome news," said Van Gogh. "Let us say you have my attention, if not my trust."

"Tell him what you told me," said Tag to Van Gogh.

"Very well," said Van Gogh. He signaled with one hand to his soldiers, who lowered their blades. Harden holstered his pistols and walked closer to the embers of the fire. "My informants tell me that Brasov is arraying forces around a former hospital in Florida. It is an armed camp. The resources diverted to this site are considerable. So considerable, in fact, that we believe what Brasov hides there must be truly unique. Yet, try as I might, I cannot determine what this thing might be. Whether it is some new weapons program, or the presence of some new, elite fighting unit, I cannot tell."

"Put all your eggs in one basket," Harden quoted, softly, "and *watch that basket.*"

"I am sorry?" said Van Gogh, confused.

"Whatever it is," said Harden. "is so important that Brasov would risk tipping his hand to guard it so overtly."

"Exactly," said Van Gogh. "You see the position this puts us in, yes?"

"Yes," said Harden. He smiled. "And I think I can help."

"Why is it you think you can help?" asked the Resistance leader.

"Because," said Harden. "I think I know what it is."

"If that is the case," said Van Gogh, "then yes, we can be friends."

Chapter Eleven

Boston

Automatic gunfire from the brownstones across the street brought down several of the human Basij, dumping them in messy heaps across the asphalt. The fools had actually fixed blades to their AK-100 rifles and attempted a bayonet charge. Ibn al Farir shook his head, laughing despite himself, and keyed his radio.

"Unit two, unit three," he said. "Move up and neutralize resistance."

Two dozen vampires separated themselves from the main column of his forces. They took the lead, arraying themselves in a skirmish line with their rifles at the ready. Four of them had RPK-74M light machineguns. These were heavier rifles fed from heavy drums of ammunition and fitted with bipods, used for extended fire. As al Farir watched, the drum-fed weapons opened up, spraying the face of the brownstones and driving the Christian heretics to cover.

Let them cower in their dens, thought al Farir. Let them return fire if they will. Their bullets will not hurt my troops.

The squads now advancing were Fedvamps detailed to bolster the Basij under Ibn al Farir's command. The extra manpower — al Farir smiled ironically to himself at the thought, but he knew of no other term — had been his specific request. The patrol of Boston was supposed to be a routine purity sweep of the Sharia enclave here, but from the first reports, al Farir had sensed treachery. For weeks, his spies within and around Boston had been reporting suspicious activity. Then, a shipment of illegal firearms had been intercepted on its way into the city. The smugglers had been tortured, but had died before giving up what they knew.

Ibn al Farir had smelled a Resistance trap.

The cleansing of infidels in the Sharia enclaves had long been a point of contention among the far-right barbarians who still insisted on fighting

Woodrow Brasov's rule. The fools had been given every opportunity to move out. For some bizarre reason, there were those among the Christians who insisted on remaining where they were. Why anyone would be attached to a building simply because their parents, or their parents' parents, had lived there in years past was a mystery to al Farir. They were Christians. This was a Muslim enclave. Therefore, they must leave or their lives were forfeit. It was as simple as that. Muslims could not be expected to coexist with the sons of dogs and pigs in their midst. It was uncivilized.

The purity sweep had been announced well in advance, as these things typically were. That had given the Resistance time to plan their trap. With their smuggled weapons, and with many men living secretly within the neighborhoods to be cleansed in the week prior to the sweep, they had lain in wait for the Basij. Purity sweeps were most often ill-planned affairs, little more than a gang of Basij with rifles and shotguns moving from door to door and rousting any nonbelievers they found. Had that been the case, the Resistance would have chopped them to pieces. It would have been a serious blow to Brasov's prestige, for the Resistance could then use the victory to promote their cause. Stand up to Brasov as we have done here, they would have proclaimed. Show him that we will not be marched from our homes. The sheer Islamophobia of it was appalling. These were men who knew nothing of their rightful place in the world. Everyone knew that infidels were less than human by definition. The creatures were fortunate Brasov had been as gentle with them as he had, up to now.

Ibn al Farir laughed at himself, laughed at his own thoughts. He was grateful he had not given voice to such women's prattling. He had been living among the infidels for far too long. How many centuries had it been since he had accompanied Altan bin Ramseur on the last of their hunting parties? It had taken centuries, but at last they had run Vlad Tepes to ground. Ibn al Farir had personally held Dracula immobile while Altan bin Ramseur delivered the *coup de grace*, separating Vlad Tepes' head from his neck and finally destroying one of Christendom's most feared warriors.

How far the infidel's faith had fallen since then.

With his Fedvamps pouring fire into the face of the building, suppressing the return fire, al Farir signaled the Basij. The human fighters moved in, eager to take their prize. The brownstones were the last pocket of resistance in this neighborhood. On realizing this al Farir felt a familiar thirst well up within him. He had not fed in battle for some weeks. It was time to do so.

"Sir," said one of the Basij, approaching him with head bowed. "A message from President Brasov." He proffered the glass oblong of his phone.

Ibn al Farir did not touch the phone. He mistrusted such technology and did not understand it, for the most part. Neither was he obligated to try; he would conduct himself according to his own will, and any man or vampire who thought otherwise would die screaming for the insolence. Still, one did not ignore messages from one's master. Al Farir's loyalty to the vampire leader of the United States was complete and total.

Report to the Florida site, read the text message. *Subject A remains reluctant. I require your special talents.*

This was not unexpected. He nodded to the Basij fighter, waving his hand for the man to take the phone away. "Send an acknowledgement," he instructed. "Inform President Brasov that I will hasten to comply once I have concluded the purity sweep."

"Yes, sir," said the Muslim militiaman. He bowed and scraped once more, backing up as if afraid to turn away, scurrying to obey his instructions.

Al Farir brought his radio to his face and keyed it once more. "Continue the attack," he said. "I am going inside."

His lieutenants knew better than to question him. It was well known that Ibn al Farir had the ear of President Woodrow Brasov himself, that al Farir answered to no one but Brasov, and that to question Ibn al Farir's actions was to risk death itself. It had been necessary to kill several men on the spot — though fewer than al Farir might have guessed — to get that point across. He was a firm believer in the dictum that it was better to be feared than loved. Brasov ruled through fear and brutality. Ibn al Farir had been an instrument of that brutality for as long as he could remember being a vampire.

A bullet struck his chest as he neared the brownstone. He ignored it. Rounding the building, he found a side door guarded by the Basij, who were trading bursts through the shattered window set within the door. On seeing al Farir, they shrunk back, bowing their heads low.

"Follow me, brothers," he told them. "Mutaween are the noblest of humans. I will shield you."

They puffed up at that, grateful for his protection and proud of the bond they shared in Allah. They were inferior, of course; all human beings were. But Mutaween were at least doing their best to fulfill the will of Allah. Technically, the Basij were the Islamic militia, while the Mutaween were those designated for purity sweeps and other enforcement actions related to Sharia law. Functionally, there was no distinction between the two. Both terms struck fear in the hearts of the infidels, which was what mattered.

The smell of blood fired al Farir's soul. He carried no weapons save an ancient Stetchkin pistol holstered at his side, the split-blade, curved *zulfiqar* sword on his back, and of course his treasured kerambit blade. He seldom needed more. Reaching out, he wrenched the door of the brownstone off its hinges, tossing it aside. Bullets struck him in the chest and face as he stroked forward, One passed through his cheek.

Snarling, streaming blood from wounds that were already closing, al Farir picked up his pace. He barreled down the corridor within, crashing through a hastily made barricade of furniture and wooden pallets. There were four Resistance fighters here, all of them armed with illegal automatic weapons. He tore through them like so much hanging meat, rending them limb from limb. He massacred all but the last man. This one he grabbed by the shoulders as the doomed infidel squirmed and cried.

"God is great!" shouted Ibn al Farir. "*Allāhu Akbar!*" A bullet squeezed from the closing wound in his forehead, falling from his face as if he wept. The infidel had time to scream once more before Ibn al Farir sank his fangs deep into the man's neck, drinking deeply. As he drank, he snapped the man's arms, delighting in the convulsions and muffled cries this elicited.

He would take his time. Before he allowed the man to die, before he drained him completely, he would break his fingers. He would pluck out his eyes one at a time. He would remove the man's teeth. He would enjoy every delicious scream, even as he drank the man's blood drop by drop. Then he would use the kerambit's keen, curved blade to gut the corpse and leave its intestines draped throughout the room. The Mutaween carried phones with cameras, devices for which Ibn al Farir had little use. They would take photos of the tableau and make sure these were distributed to the media. All who opposed the will of Allah would learn the futility of such a crime.

The thought brought a smile to his face as he enjoyed his battlefield meal. God was great, indeed.

* * *

The Blue Ridge Mountains

"We will need more weaponry," said Van Gogh. He used a piece of bread to sop up the last of the campfire-cooked stew his troops had prepared. The campfire around which they sat — on compact folding sling-chairs furnished by the Resistance — was larger than Harden would have thought advisable, but Van Gogh knew his business. He had posted guards far from the campsite to make sure nothing and no one approached them.

Harden poked at his food politely, holding the aluminum camp tin with one hand and sipping from a borrowed canteen with the other. He had fed deeply on the whitetail deer overnight; he would not need much to eat or drink for some time. Still, he did not want Van Gogh to think the Resistance's hospitality was not appreciated. Thanks to Tag vouching for him, and Van Gogh's own knowledge of the Cousinry's history of contributions to the cause, it had been a relatively easy thing to commit to working together.

Things had been a bit tense at first, especially given the fact that Harden was a vampire. Most of the vampires with whom the Resistance interacted directly were Fedvamps enforcing Brasov's iron-fisted rule. To them, the Cousinry vampires were a theory only, creatures they had been told about but with whom they had no direct experience. Sitting around a campfire with one had taken a little adjusting. But thanks to Tag's easy familiarity with the Resistance, Harden's own direct nature, and the very real necessity of finding a way to defeat Brasov, they had gotten through the initial awkwardness.

Harden looked up, catching Tag staring at him from across the fire. It struck him, then, just how beautiful she was. He tried to push the thought away, tried to focus on his conversation with Van Gogh. For the first time, he noticed just how tightly the old tiger stripe BDU blouse she wore clung to her body. She wore a black tank top beneath it that was just as taut. The curve of her neck, the hollow of her throat, the high cheekbones of her exquisite face... she was strikingly attractive in a way he not fully appreciated before.

Blood, he thought. With his body fully fed, healed, and rested, his senses were turning to... other things. A vampire's libido was always at its highest after he had fed properly.

It was Tag who turned away first. Was she blushing? He couldn't tell, but he thought he'd seen her smile at him before she did. She was chatting with a few of the other Resistance soldiers, their voices low. Noise discipline was something the Resistance men and women had been forced to learn early on. Vampires had excellent hearing that extended far beyond the audible range that humans possessed. Staying quiet, even when reasonably certain they were safe, was habitual among Van Gogh's people.

"Will manpower be a problem?" asked Harden.

"No," said Van Gogh. "Manpower I have. Vehicles I have. Why, I even have a pair of old Boeing helicopters and pilots to fly them. Every day, more people look to the Resistance for answers. Brasov is tightening his grip. The ranks of our people are swelling. A storm is coming and the people perceive it. But if we are to stage a raid on a hardened site guarded by Fedvamps, we will need more firepower than we now possess."

The hardened site was the address in Florida on which Van Gogh's spies had reported. It had once been a mental hospital, though this was reported closed decades previously. It was once again thanks to Thomas Simpson's foresight that Harden knew, or thought he knew, what Brasov could be guarding. It was the culmination of centuries of hunting on Brasov's part, again as recorded in Simpson's journal.

"There's a Federal Armory outside Tampa," said Harden. "Can you get us and your team into position there?"

"I can," said Van Gogh. "But we've thought about hitting government arms stores before. Every time we've tried in the past, we have lost good people and gained nothing for it."

"I'll help you plan the raid," said Harden. "I've had time to build up some military experience."

Van Gogh looked at him for a long moment. "Yes," he said. "I imagine you would." He looked away for a moment, surveying the campsite, before turning back to Harden. "She wants you," he said softly.

Harden raised an eyebrow. "Pardon me?"

Van Gogh chuckled. "She is a good woman," he said. "Brave. She thinks of herself as nothing but a smuggler, but she has the soul of a freedom fighter. You are a lucky man."

"I'm not a *man* at all," said Harden quietly. "I'm a vampire."

"You are, I think, a man in every way that matters," said Van Gogh. "Enough. I must sleep. We will meet the trucks in the morning. The route to Florida will have to be indirect. The trip will be long. But with your help, we will succeed."

* * *

Harden checked over his pack, with its large bedroll slung at the bottom. He had salvaged everything he needed from the Ford, including his personal weapons. The items he could not carry he had distributed among the Resistance members, an act that seemed to buy him instant goodwill among several of them. The Mustang smart-car was damaged enough by gunfire that it made more sense to leave it here. With Van Gogh's help, he had rigged a couple of camouflage tarps over it, tying them to ground stakes. When next he made his way back to Georgia, he would recover the car if it was possible. The centuries had taught him that material possessions were largely disposable, but he was still attached to some of them. His vintage WWII 1911s were in his pack, for example, as was Thomas' precious journal.

The secret the journal imparted had kept the whole camp spellbound as Harden read selections aloud from it to tell the tale. The only thing valuable enough to draw so much of Brasov's attention was a prize the vampire dictator had been seeking for centuries. Cousinry spies had documented the hunt for Adam, fabled among their kind as the very first of the undead.

Vampires, after all, were never born. They were always made. Adam was rumored to be the first of their kind. The secret of his origin could reveal the secret of how vampires came to be. That knowledge, Brasov believed, was the key to absolute power over vampire kind. For example, knowing how Adam had become a vampire might lead to a means of "curing" vampirism. In the hands of Woodrow Brasov, that would be a powerful weapon.

Already, Brasov held a considerable amount of sway among vampires on a direct and personal level. Brasov himself cultivated the rumors that he was originally Vlad Tepes, the infamous warrior known as the Impaler. Giving such a man control over the very existence of vampire kind would only make him that much more difficult to defeat. It could not be allowed to happen. Through the years, the Cousinry had tried to stymie Brasov's efforts to locate Adam. This task was complicated by the fact that nobody, not even Cousinry historians, were entirely certain that Adam existed. Some thought he had been various famous historical figures, each time faking his death and moving on to another persona. Others thought he was a myth concocted by vampires to explain the origin of their existence. Still others theorized that if Adam were himself a vampire, someone must have turned him millennia ago.

Harden had read many of these accounts, and discussed the possibility of Adam's existence many times with Thomas. The pair had come to the conclusion that there were too many historical references for Adam to be fictitious. Sightings were numerous; sifting the real ones from the false ones had vexed Cousinry scholars for hundreds of years. Now, though, it seemed likely that Brasov had found the vampire for whom he had so desperately sought. Adam's alleged history went back millennia, far beyond the dawn of recorded history. The wisdom such a being might hold was a wonder to contemplate. If he were being held in Florida, freeing him might prove a tremendous advantage to the Resistance. And if Brasov had found Adam and Adam now worked with Brasov and the Fedvamps, eliminating him might be the only way to prevent Brasov from vastly increasing his power over vampire kind.

There was a third possibility, which was that Adam was not the subject of Brasov's attention in Florida. If that were the case, they still needed to know what was hidden there. The raid must be conducted regardless. The only question was whether the losses they were likely to suffer would be worth it. Attacking a hardened federal site was risky even for a fully equipped military force. For the Resistance, even bolstered with the weapons Harden planned to help them steal, it might be suicide.

He was not overly fatigued, but the rest of the camp was growing still as the other Resistance fighters bedded down for the night. He considered untying his heavy bedroll from the pack. Even if he did not sleep, he could mull over plans for the armory attack and quiet his mind in preparation for the work to come. Centuries of battle had taught him that you had to take these quiet times when they were available. You would not always have the luxury.

He heard Tag before she became visible in the flicker of the distant camp-fire. Harden had positioned himself far from the others to avoid disturbing them while he went through his things. Now Tag knelt next to him, spreading her borrowed bedroll on the ground next to his pack. She had a pack of her own, now, provided by Van Gogh, who had also scrounged up some BDUs that would fit her. She put her Thompson on the ground, gently, leaning it against her pack.

"Hey," said Harden.

"Hey," said Tag.

"Look—" she started to say.

"I was thinking—" Harden said at the same time. They both laughed, soft-ly, trying not to disturb the others. "Ladies first," he said.

Tag regarded him in the dwindling firelight. "Watching you out there, on the road," she said. "And before, at Thomas' house. I've never seen anything like it."

"I've been watching you, too," he admitted.

"I don't have any experience with vampires," Tag said frankly. "Thomas was the only one I talked to regularly, not counting customers. I don't know how this works for you." She kicked off her boots and slid into her bedroll. There was a little commotion as she moved around inside it, her legs pushing the cloth to its limit. Then her arm emerged and she put her pants on top of her pack."

"It works the same way as it does with anybody else," said Harden. He removed his boots.

"I think there's room in here for both of us," said Tag.

"You think so?"

"Yeah," she said. He thought he could see her blushing again, slightly, as he squeezed into the bedroll with her. The warmth of her body against him was electric.

"You're sure?" he said.

"I'm sure," she said. Her tone was almost teasing. "I read a book on vampires once. It said you were... 'dysfunctional,' I think the word was. That vampires couldn't get it up."

"That's very wrong," said Harden. He slid his hand under her BDU blouse, feeling her taut stomach under his palm. She closed her eyes and exhaled, her breath hot on his face.

"Show me," she whispered.

Chapter Twelve

Florida

Adam opened his eyes. The room in which he now found himself was almost surgically clean, gleaming white and smelling of ancient antiseptic. He was bound at the wrists and ankles with steel cable, securing him to the gurney on which he rested. He wore only a paper hospital gown. He was not sure how much time had passed while he languished in the poisoned chamber. With nothing to eat, and with no way to tell time, one day had blended into the next, as his sleep cycles came whenever his exhausted mind and body could manage an hour or two of slumber. He felt parched, dried out, a desiccated husk waiting to be split open. His throat was so dry he was not sure he would be able to speak.

Movement in the room caught his attention. He tried to turn his head, but he had been strapped down at the neck as well. A powerful hand clamped down on his left arm. He groaned.

"Drink," said a deep voice. The mouth of a plastic bottle of water was placed at his lips. The water was not what he wanted, not what he needed, but he accepted it anyway, feeling the liquid soak the thick weight of his tongue and soothe the back of his throat. He swallowed with difficulty. The steel cable over his throat was very tight.

"Greetings," said the man. He was immense and muscular, dark of complexion, with a thick beard and even, white teeth — even, that is, save for his massive fangs. He was a vampire, but then, Adam had been able to sense that even before he could see the man. The vampire wore black leather pants tucked into high boots and a black "commando" turtleneck of a type Adam had seen before. A handgun of some kind was holstered on his hip.

"Hello," Adam croaked. His voice sounded strange to him.

"Forgive the ignorance of those who have interrogated you up to now," said the man. "I could have told them these methods, the chamber with the gas... these would not be effective on one such as you. I have had you removed from the chamber so that I may see to your care personally."

"You will," said Adam, his throat raw, "pardon me if I seem ungrateful."

"I am Ibn al Farir," said the big man. "I am the personal lieutenant and most trusted aide of President Woodrow Brasov."

"The man who stole Vlad Tepes' name," said Adam.

Al Farir looked surprised, then tried to cover the expression. He realized too late his failure. His expression became one of chagrin. "And how do you claim to know such a thing?"

"I knew Vlad Tepes," said Adam. "I have known many vampires. I heard the rumors of Dracula's death... and then new rumors, that he had survived. By then, few who had met him personally remained alive to say otherwise. But I did. Brasov is an imposter, taking the name of Dracula to further his ambitions. I have known many like him."

"So I imagine you have," said Farir. "You know what I am yes?"

"A torturer," said Adam. "A brigand. An enforcer. A monster. Those such as Brasov always keep creatures such as you close to hand... until they do not need them any longer. If you are not killed in battle, Ibn al Farir, you will be killed at the hand of the master you serve."

"Then I shall go gladly," said al Farir, "for it will mean I go to Allah with a pure heart."

Adam closed his eyes. He said nothing for a moment. Then he said, "Ask your questions. Perform your torture. It will make no difference."

"All vampires are made," said al Farir. "This is known. It is accepted. Even in ancient times, your name was spoken. The first of us. The oldest of us. My master, as you call him, has searched for you for a very long time. Almost more obsessively than he searched for Vlad Tepes."

"Revenge," said Adam, his eyes still closed. "Brasov wanted revenge on Dracula."

"You know this?"

"No," said Adam. "I know vampires. I know men. It is the only motive that explains his actions through the centuries. His obsessive pursuit of Vlad Tepes."

"You claim not to remember," said al Farir. "Yet you remember so much that has transpired among our kind. Every piece of vampire literature speaks of you in some way. Our progenitor. The first of the undead. You must know how you were created. You must have the key to vampire kind. This secret will make President Brasov very powerful."

"President Brasov is already very powerful," said Adam. "That is the thing about taking power. There is never enough of it for those who do."

Al Farir sneered. "Enough," he said. "I wish to show you something." He drew from his waistband a folding knife that snapped open automatically as he drew it. He held it in a reverse grip, his index finger through a ring in the handle. The blade was wickedly curved, like scythe. "This is a folding kerambit. It is a fine weapon, native to Southeast Asia. It excels, among other things, when gutting one's prey."

"I have seen many weapons in my life," said Adam.

"So you have," said al Farir. "Clearly you were unmoved by the impersonal methods used on you to this point. I can understand that. My... colleagues... are not so adept at prying information from the unwilling as am I. Their methods are crude. You should be flattered, Adam. This facility, the resources deployed to protect it... all were put in place to house and protect you."

"To hold me prisoner," said Adam. "When your Federal vampires found me in Tibet I told them then that I cannot answer their questions."

"Because you do not wish to help President Brasov?"

"Because I do not remember," said Adam. "I have lived *lifetimes*, Ibn al Farir. I have lived for countless millennia. I remember walking the Earth when mortal men drew on cave walls. I brought them *fire*, al Farir. I showed them how to use it to harden their weapons and to cook their food. Do you comprehend how long ago that was?"

"Thousands of years," said al Farir. "Surely."

"Thousands of thousands," said Adam. "My birth, my creation, my... genesis... was so long ago that I do not remember it. I have simply been, for as long as I can remember. There is no secret, Al Farir. There is nothing I can give your master because I do not know the answer itself. I know only what I have seen of vampire kind through those millennia. I know our capacity to destroy ourselves. I know the futility of war with human kind. I know the dangerous arrogance of believing ourselves superior. In my time, al Farir, I have seen humans nearly hunt us to extinction. And it is by my hand that our kind lived again when we reached that precipice. You may well be descended from those I turned... vampires I created to prevent us being burned from the face of the world."

"Then it is *you* who will have to pardon *me*," said al Farir. He brought the curved blade of the kerambit close to Adam's face. "For I, too, may seem ungrateful."

"And that is because?" said Adam, although he knew the answer already.

"A vampire's ability to heal is among his greatest strengths," said Al Farir. "But when he is put to the knife, when he is questioned under duress, this becomes his greatest liability. This is because pain, Adam, knows no boundaries. An eye that restores itself after it has been cut out can be cut out a second time, and a third, until the exquisite agony of the experience brings him to the brink of madness. Perhaps, even, over its edge."

"I believe you."

"Oh," said Ibn al Farir, "you do not have to take my word for it. Let me show you."

* * *

Florida

Van Gogh was a passionate leader, but he was not the most able tactician. Harden had realized that within the first few minutes of planning out the assault on the federal armory. The armory itself was a cinder block box constructed during the Cold War, sitting behind a square perimeter fence topped with razor wire. The area in which it was situated was so remote that only a dirt and gravel road — more dirt than gravel, now — led to the facility. Stands of trees and undergrowth that might once have been cleared had been allowed to overgrow the surrounding property. This would give them some concealment as they approached the armory.

Harden had devised a plan that would hopefully keep the worst of the federal defenses off them. These consisted mostly of sandbag emplacements with Squad Automatic Weapons and two-man teams, one gunner and one rifle-equipped spotter for each. The guns were placed at the four corners of the armory within the fence line. That meant that an approaching enemy would need to deal with the fence while the machineguns inside the perimeter cut them to pieces.

It was unlikely there would be landmines or other obstacles before the perimeter. This was Florida, not Vietnam, and the federal forces were not accustomed to having their facilities directly assaulted. The show of force that was the gun emplacements was typically enough to scare off Resistance cells, who lacked the motivation or the cohesion to take down such a hardened site. At least, that was how Harden interpreted what Van Gogh had told him.

Van Gogh, for his part, seemed buoyed by Harden's presence. He had embraced Harden's plan enthusiastically. It reminded Harden of something Thomas had told him.

Hope is first, Thomas had said more than once. *Everything else flows from that.*

He and Tag had also discussed with Van Gogh precisely what they must look for once they breached the armory. The Resistance had small arms, including what was almost a surplus of AK100 rifles. The arms had been produced extensively by Chinese manufacturers on government contract to the United States once the US Military switched to the AKM platform. That meant that rifles were plentiful on the black market. While more ammunition was always welcome, what Van Gogh and his people needed, and what they hoped to distribute to other Resistance cells, were rocket propelled grenades, mortars, plastic explosives, next-generation Claymore mines, and anti-tank/anti-air arms. With these, they would stand a chance against the armored troop carriers and anti-personnel patrol machinery that Brasov's Fedvamps typically employed.

The Resistance stood little chance, for example, against Fedvamp patrols traveling in Mine Resistant Ambush Protected armored trucks. The MRAPs, some of them military surplus that was decades old, were still very potent vehicles. Often they were equipped with mounted weaponry, from .50 caliber machineguns to flamethrowers to missile pods. The vehicles were also equipped with jamming equipment to prevent the detonation of improvised explosive devices, technology that went all the way back to what Brasov's administration called New Crusades — the Iraq and Afghanistan campaigns at the turn of the twenty-first century. Brasov had made quite a production of apologizing to the Muslim world, formally in a ceremony at the People's White House, for the transgressions of American troops during those "crusades." He had no qualms, nonetheless, about using the technology of those wars in his efforts to control and suppress American freedom.

Harden, Tag, and the other Resistance fighters wore their full packs. Mobility was essential in an operation like this. There would be no going back for supplies or arms left behind. Harden had his holstered pistols, his toma-hawk, and a borrowed AK100. He wore his canvas shoulder bag over his chest to carry extra magazines and drop his empties. In a drop-leg holster borrowed from one of the Resistance members, he had strapped the MAC-11. He was, in other words, loaded for bear, but his vampire strength meant that he barely noticed the weight.

For her part, Tag, had insisted on keeping her Thompson to hand. It was the weapon with which she was most familiar and thus would serve her best in combat. Harden did not particularly like the idea of taking her into battle in this way, but there was no other choice.

Tag. Thoughts of her now pervaded his thoughts and he had to force him-self to focus on the task at hand. When the dawn came they had not spent much time discussing what had occurred the night before, but there had been no need. A very real understanding lay between them now. She met his eyes as Harden and Van Gogh gathered near the cab of the sacrifice truck. He smiled at her and she did the same, throwing him a thumbs up.

Van Gogh was surveying the gun emplacements with a pair of thermal bin-oculars. He took the device from his eyes and looked to Harden. "Heat signa-tures are all too low for humans," he reported. "Those are Fedvamps down there, every last one of them. The ones posted outside, anyway."

That made sense. Brasov would not trust the storage of his weapons to mere human beings, whose loyalty might be to their country first. It was why Brasov was pouring so many American troops into pointless, losing, underfunded wars overseas. Here at home, he could control his vampire legions. The Fedvamps were his private army, owing their immortality to Brasov and his agents. Woodrow Brasov was the only ideal in which they believed, not the tenets of liberty on which the United States Constitution had been written.

"Nothing to stop us, then," said Harden. He felt his jaw work as he considered the damage Brasov and his forces had done to the United States in the last few decades. "Let's go."

"Yes," Van Gogh agreed. "We can commence."

Harden nodded. He climbed up into the truck. Tag now looked worried, but Harden shook his head. "Stubborn, remember?" he said. "Don't worry." She probably couldn't hear him from where he stood, but she would be able to read his lips. She inclined her chin at him and Harden was once again struck by her beauty.

Focus, he told himself. *Work now, play later.*

"It is a brave thing you do," said Van Gogh

"Not really," said Harden. "It'd be a lot braver if you did it. For obvious reasons."

"I do not wish to trade," said Van Gogh, laughing softly. He held up a heavy-duty bush machete. "I sharpened this myself. You will need it. Your tomahawk will not be enough.

"Thank you," said Harden. He stowed the machete inside the truck. "Let's roll."

Van Gogh nodded and hefted the RPG launcher he carried. At his signal, his troops spread out among the trees and scrub, crouching down with their rifles at their shoulders.

Harden went to the cab of the truck. It was an old military surplus hauler, similar to the deuce-and-a-half vehicles he had driven in Europe and Korea in the forties and fifties, or the M35 6X6 trucks that had replaced those. As war-torn as the last half-century had been, there was always lots of military surplus on the market, both domestic and foreign production. Well, Harden thought. It was *all* foreign production, really. Even companies still considered nominally American manufacturers made all their products overseas and shipped them in, including the equipment used by the overextended, poorly funded United States military.

"Remember," said Harden. "As soon as I hit the fence, get your men moving to the opposite corner. If it's electrified, my collision should play hell with the field, but don't assume it's not still hot when your people hit it."

"We have insulated bayonets," Van Gogh said, grinning. "Standard AK100 equipment. They will double as wire cutters to get us through the fence."

"That will work," said Harden. He climbed into the truck. Van Gogh threw him a final thumbs up and ran off to join Tag and his men.

Harden sat behind the wheel. This was it. He was committed, now; there was no turning back. He had bent the law many times as a member of the Cousinry, had circumvented the ever-crawling, every growing, ever-tighter web of Brasov's unconstitutional laws. He had watched as the America he knew, the America he had fought for, turned into something he could not recognize. He was now about to engage in an open act of war against Brasov's government. He had agreed with funding the Resistance before; he had retained arms that Brasov's government had declared illegal; he had done everything in his power to quietly stand up against the massive illegal machine the Social Democrats had built from the United States government. But this was different. This was open, armed devices. This was insurrection. This was sedition.

This was the right thing to do.

Feeling more at peace with himself than he had in years, Harden fired up the old truck, shifted into low gear, and tromped the gas pedal. It felt good to be behind the wheel of something so old, something that predated the modern madness of the world. The deuce-and-half rumbled out of the tree line and roared toward the armory, heading for the southeast corner. There was nothing particular strategic about that corner; it was simply the one closest to Harden's position.

He was a little worried about the ground he was traversing; if it was too soft, if the truck bogged down, he would be a sitting duck while the plan would not work. Well, there was that old saying. No plan survives first contact with the enemy...

The truck, however, did not bog down. It took longer than he would have thought for the guards to notice his approach. It might have been that they were getting clearance to fire. Brasov's foreign rules of engagement were notorious for the limits they put on American soldiers.

Faster, he thought. *More speed. Pick up as much momentum as you can. You'll need it.* He began working the gear shift as the truck accelerated. The engine howled, threatening to tear itself apart. The old beast hadn't been pushed this long in a while, perhaps ever. He was going to blow the engine if he didn't ease down.

It wouldn't matter.

The SAW gunners behind the sandbag emplacements opened up. They were firing on full auto, every few rounds a bright red tracer that streaked toward Harden like something out of a space opera.

A round punched through the windshield. Then another. Then a third. Once he was in range of the adjacent corner, that emplacement opened up, too. Soon rounds from both SAWs were tearing into the deuce-and-a-half, ripping it apart. He felt round after round smash through the cabin of the truck. Trying to make himself as small a target as possible, he crouched down behind the wheel. Some of the incoming fire still found him. A round drilled through his thigh. Another punched through his chest. Then two more drilled through his sternum. Yet another grazed his forehead. As he turned, a hot round sizzled through his face, blowing a hole from one cheek through to the other. Teeth and blood sprayed the compartment.

This is going to hurt, he thought.

The deuce-and-a-half struck the fence and then plowed through the gun emplacement, crushing the Fedvamps and their SAW beneath its shredded tires. When it finally came to rest, Harden shrugged on his pack and stumbled out of the vehicle. He had the heavy machete in hand and, as the broken bodies of the Fedvamps squirmed, he went to each vampire and severed his head from his neck.

A bullet popped from his chest, followed by a second. The pain was... memorable.

Still a little fuzzy on his feet, Harden ran for the second emplacement. Van Gogh's people were streaming in through the broken fence now, fanning out and laying down suppressing fire. Harden reached the next SAW nest first. He took a burst through the thighs that nearly chopped his legs out from under him, but his momentum carried him past the sandbags. He dropped his machete, drew his Commanders, and blasted both vampires directly in the face several times. While they were struggling to deal with several heavy lead hollow-points in their brains, Harden was able to retrieve his machete, limp to each of them, and chop their heads off.

The automatic gunfire going off around him was very heavy now. He thought he could recognize the heavy, spirited thump of Tag's Tommy gun among the hollow metallic clatter of the AK100s. The Kalashnikov had evolved through the years, but the sound would always be distinctive. It made him remember the jungles of Vietnam...

No! he told himself. *Don't give in to the blood loss. Don't get distracted.*

He was healing, but he still needed a little time. No human member of Van Gogh's Resistance would have been able to survive that assault. Harden realized he almost had not, either. Around him, Van Gogh's troops were already seeing to their work. he was tempted to wander off, to let the confusion take him, but suddenly Tag was there. Her beautiful face brought him back to the here and now. She smiled at him, took, his arm, and guided him to cover as the Resistance fighters flowed around them. Their rifles fired and fired.

Van Gogh did not have much in the way of explosives, but he had scraped together everything he could. It would be enough to blow the door. It would have to be.

It was.

Harden, still recovering from his wounds, felt as if he were floating along, being carried by his own momentum and by Tag's warm hand. He followed her through the breached door of the armory. There was more gunfire, striking the wall all around them. Instinctively, Harden grabbed Tag and pulled her close, pivoting to put himself between her and the enemy. More bullets struck his back, punishing his body, driving him down into blackness.

"Harden!" shouted Tag. "HARDEN!"

Chapter Thirteen

South Vietnam, November, 1965

The first major battle between the United States 1/7 Air Cavalry Battalion and the People's Army of Vietnam took place during Operation Silver Bayonet. The airmobile offensive was part of a large campaign, Operation Long Reach. The battle of la Drang, named for a river running through the valley west of Plei Me where the action occurred, would result in heavy casualties over two days. Before it was all over, the United States had lost 250 men. As many as a thousand North Vietnamese soldiers had fallen to gunfire, while yet more may have been destroyed by artillery and air support. There were those who called it an ambush. Still others called it a kind of qualified victory for the North Vietnamese. The United States military was, arguably, not prepared for the ferocity of the battle that occurred, or for the heavy losses it sustained.

Vincent Harden did not give one good damn about any of that.

Tossing his helmet aside, he found Private Stillman among the cleanup crews. Then he grabbed Stillman by the collar, threw him to the ground, leapt on top of him, and proceeded to beat him unconscious with his fists.

Stillman was a coward, the kind of soldier who ran from battle and who rifled through the pockets of his fellow Americans after they died. Harden had seen it during the heat of battle — something he would not have believed if he hadn't witnessed it himself. He had made a note to find Stillman after the battle. Found him he had.

Powerful hands separated the two of them. Nobody liked Stillman; nobody was going to report this. Harden was still kicking and punching as he was dragged off his foe. He could easily have fought them all, but they were his brothers. Only Stillman warranted his wrath.

He still remembered the voices of the soldiers who had finally pulled him off Stillman. Fortunately for him, they did it before he killed the bastard. To this day, Harden was not sure if he would have taken Stillman's life... but he wanted to. He wanted to very much.

"Harden! Harden! HARDEN!" shouted the soldiers.

* * *

Florida

"I'm okay," said Harden. He knelt down in the corridor with Tag covering him. Her knuckles were white on the grips of her Thompson. "Just took me a minute to come back from that."

"You're sure? You can move?"

"I can move," said Harden. "Lead the way."

"Maybe you should lead," she said, shooting him a lopsided grin. "Stubborn, remember?"

"Yeah," he said. "Stubborn." He had lost his Kalashnikov along the way. Wait, had he had one? Was it back at the truck? He shook his head. He must have taken a round through the brain somewhere along the way; it was the only explanation for his fuzzy-headedness. No time to worry about it now. He had his pistols, he had his tomahawk on his belt, and he had the machete someone had given him. Van Gogh. The machete Van Gogh had given him. That was it.

It would be enough.

Taking the lead, Harden held his pistol high and compressed. The machete, in his left hand, felt solid. He was ready. His head was clearing. He was taking the battle to Brasov's minions.

That felt good.

The corridors here in the armory were tight, block on block, coated in institutional paint the color of spoiled milk. Fighting here would be at close quarters; the enemy might be on top of them before they knew—

The Fedvamps came snarling and barreling up the corridor, shrugging off the automatic gunfire of Van Gogh's troops. Harden braced himself as the lead vampire crashed into him, driving him to the floor. He put a pair of .45 slugs through the vampire's eyes, rolled, and popped up again. A bullet struck him in the shoulder above his pack, but it wasn't bad. He chopped off the head of the vampire on the floor and almost slipped in the geyser of blood that spewed forth.

"Behind you!" Tag shouted. Her "Chicago typewriter" smoked and chugged, the stream of heavy rounds chopping the knees out from under the onrushing vamps.

Smart, thought Harden. Tag had good combat instincts and no lack of courage.

Van Gogh edged up next to Harden. He had his radio in his hand. "My men report that the jammer is holding," he said. "They're ready to bring the trucks in as soon as we have pacified the defense forces."

"We need to find the radio room," said Harden. "If they manage to get through, we'll have gunships or jets down on us before we can move the weapons out."

"Let's try up ahead and to the left," said Van Gogh.

"Just hurry," urged Harden.

* * *

Eurasia, 600,000 B.C.

The tribe was angry. There had been no food; the hunt had produced nothing. They huddled together for warmth beneath the dubious shelter of the outcropping. The wind was cold. The rain had been colder. Already, another of their number was very sick. He would see three or four more sunrises at most.

Adam spread his hands, trying not to alarm them. He knew he looked different, compared to them. He knew they would find his clothing strange, his ways stranger. But he approached nonetheless. The length of bush he held was burning steadily, despite the wind. The tribe saw the fire and shrank back.

There were no words he could share with them; he did not speak their language. He did not speak *any* language; he thought in pictures, in urges, in concepts. He had no need to share his thoughts with others. There had never been any others for him to communicate with or to. No others like himself. No others who lived solely by drinking the blood of lesser creatures. No others who, like Adam, did not grow older, did not get sick, and did not die. If he stumbled and cut his hand, the cut healed immediately. If he slept more than a tiny portion of every night, he was not aware of it. Adam knew he was somehow different from the other beings struggling to survive. He could not explain that difference, nor was there anyone to whom he might explain it.

Adam was alone.

He gathered brush and dead wood as best he could, built a campfire, and found one of the four-legged beasts nearby, a creature not quite fast enough to evade him. He killed it, skinned it with the sharp nails of his hands, and roasted the creature. The smell of food brought the tribe out of hiding. They approached, furtive, wary, holding heavy rocks with which they might crush his skull if he gave them reason.

He gave them no reason to fight. Instead, he gave them food — cooked food, something new to them. They ate it happily once he demonstrated. A full belly made all the difference. Soon, he and the tribe were friends, at least for the moment.

The tribe had left their sick member by the outcropping. Adam pointed, tried to make them understand. They were not sure how to interpret his gestures. He had no way to tell them that he wanted to help. The sick did not get better. The sick grew sicker until they died. They had never seen someone healed from ill health.

Adam crept forward. The tribe watched, their meal momentarily forgotten. They did not understand. But he would show them.

He bared his fangs. They started; there were dangerous beasts with similar teeth. He bit deeply into the sick tribesman's neck. This, they accepted. The sick were good for little else. Who were they to argue with this strange newcomer's choice of meal?

Adam ripped open his own wrist with his teeth. He placed his arm over the dying tribesman's face. Soon, the tribesman was drinking eagerly from Adam's veins. Not long after that, he was healed. He opened his eyes. He stood. He stared at Adam in disbelief.

Adam, too, disbelieved. He had done it by instinct. He had not known why; he had simply done what seemed natural. Now he knew the truth. He had the power to heal. He would travel the world, healing other tribes, bringing them the gift of fire—

Something came over the tribesman's face. He opened his mouth, revealing fangs of his own. Whirling, he spotted his tribe by the fire. He snarled.

He leapt.

As Adam wailed in horror, the tribesman set upon his fellows, murdering each one of them and drinking their blood. He did not stop until they were all dead... and then he turned his bloody face to Adam.

"No," said Adam. "No. No!"

* * *

Florida

"Wake up," said Ibn al Farir. "You were dreaming. Speaking in your sleep. What does one as old as you dream? Tell me."

Adam's eyes fluttered open. The pain was still very intense. His eyelids were still growing back. He had not fed for a very long time and the process was slow.

"What... What did I say?"

"You said 'no,'" al Farir sneered. "This does not help me. The pain will not end, Adam, until you reveal your secrets. If I have to drag your intestines out of your body and down the hallway, I shall. We have not tried that yet. But we will if you do not tell me your secrets."

Adam struggled weakly. "Do what you must," he said.

"I will feed you blood," said al Farir. "I will bring you to the brink of death and then bring you back. Your pain will never stop."

"I will not drink," said Adam. "Never again."

Ibn al Farir scoffed. "Are you one of them? The pacifists, who believe we should deny the thirst that defines our nature?"

"I have lived too long," said Adam. "I have seen too much."

"Weakling," said al Farir. "I have lived long. I have seen much. I have killed. I have raped. I have burned whole villages to the earth on which they stood. I have fought the forces of Christendom, the chaos of Western individualism, for as long as I can remember. Never have I surrendered the way you have. I do not understand you Western men. You lack strength. You lack conviction."

"I am not a Western man," said Adam. "I am no man. I am no one."

"Fool," said al Farir. "You are like all of them. Why do you think Brasov has succeeded? Why do you think he has risen to power? He is strong. The West is weak. These pitiful Social Democrats were only too willing to give a dictator like Brasov control over their pitiful lives. As weaklings, they craved strength. They craved leadership. And so desperate were they to see their own excesses curbed, their own whims and wanton desires held in check, that they embraced Brasov's reforms. They embraced the destruction of their own pathetic 'liberties.' They willingly voted to subjugate their fellow human beings. Your kind will never survive because secretly you crave your own destruction. You *beg* to become slaves. And when Brasov declares global Sharia, you will become so, once and for all."

"There is nothing I can tell you," said Adam, closing his stunted eyelids. Tracks of salt, created by the uncontrolled watering of his eyes, had left streaks of white down both sides of his face. "There is nothing I remember about my origin that Brasov can use. I am not a weapon. I am a disease."

"Weak," said al Farir. "Now I am going to start cutting off your fingers. We will see how long it takes them to grow back this time."

* * *

The fighting was brutal and bloody, but with Harden leading them, they were able to make quick work of the defenders. Once guards had been put in place, Van Gogh called for the other trucks to be brought up. Now he and his men were loading the weapons they would need, while the guards stood ready to alert them to Fedvamp reinforcements.

"There wasn't a human being among them," said Tag.

Harden was standing near the front door of the armory. He had been staring at the tree line, thinking. At her approach, he nodded.

"No," said Harden. "There are more and more Fedvamps every day. Brasov is turning them to build an army. He's going to use them, and the Basij, to take complete control."

"Isn't he already in complete control?"

"President for Life does seem fairly final," said Harden. "But dictator isn't enough for someone like Brasov. You can hear it every time he gives a national address. There's still too many of us who don't conform to his idea of proper behavior among his subjects. A few of us still have the gall to disagree with him or, worse, to fight against him."

"Do you ever wonder if he's Dracula?"

Harden shook his head. "I know the rumor. I've never given it much thought. Thomas Simpson didn't think so. He thought Brasov cultivated the rumor to draw support from our kind. Dracula was something of a legend among vampires, and not in the way humans think of him. He was like Hawkins, only much more so. A cult of personality many found irresistible."

"Isn't that Brasov, though? A cult of personality?"

"Sure," said Harden. "But Dracula fought *for* Christianity and against the Muslim Turks. Brasov hates Christians and has repeatedly fought to crush Christian freedom in the United States. He actively promotes Muslim causes abroad. Creating the Sharia enclaves was his way of establishing Muslim beachheads here within U.S. soil. Thomas spoke often about it. It bothered him very much."

"It bothers *me* very much," said Tag.

"I know," said Harden. "Me, too."

She looked up at him. He was still staring at the tree line as if he'd never seen it before.

"You okay?" she asked. "Something wrong?"

"I feel like I wasted an awful lot of time," said Harden. "I feel like I should have been pushing Thomas to bring the Cousinry into the fight long before now. It took his death to get me to see it. I wanted to do things slowly.

Gradually. I wanted to work behind the scenes. But really... Really I think I was avoiding getting involved in the world again."

"When did you stop?"

"After Vietnam," said Harden. "It... shook me. In a way that previous wars did not. I tried to hide from the world. Tried to have it both ways. It took Thomas' suicide to get me back in the fight."

"Have you ever thought maybe Thomas knew that, too?" said Tag. "Maybe... maybe he did what he had to do for *you*. And for the future."

"Maybe he did," said Harden, nodding. "Maybe he did, at that. If so, I owe him a great deal. But there's a lot more to do yet. A lot more fighting before we stop."

"I'm ready if you are," said Tag.

He turned to her on impulse, grabbed her, and pressed his lips to hers. She melted into him as they kissed. Before he pulled away again, he reached up and ran his fingers through her closely bobbed hair.

"Yeah," he said. "I'm ready."

"Then let's get to work," she told him.

Chapter Fourteen

Misenum, 37 A.D.

Aeliana handed Caligula the pillow. "He's still alive," she said.

Qintus Naevius Sutorius Macro, prefect of the Praetorian Guard, lent his weight to the pillow. Together with Caligula, they held the pillow over Tiberius' face long after he stopped struggling. When it was finally done, Macro left, knowing Aeliana and Caligula would want time alone.

"I want you," he told her. "I will take you over his dead body."

Aeliana nodded. It was not the worst thing she would let him do — and nothing compared to the hell that had been living as the consort, the sexual plaything, of Tiberius Claudius Nero. Now that Nero was dead, his political capital gone, the way was clear for Caligula to take control of Rome. Tiberius' will ceded power jointly to Caligula — his adopted son and grand-nephew — and Tiberius' blood grandson Gemellus. It would be a simple matter to murder Gemellus. Caligula was utterly infatuated with Aeliana, and not entirely stable. It was at her urging that he had finally taken action to put his grand-uncle down for good. Caligula was not entirely stable at the best of times. His appetites ruled him. It was why she could use him.

Tiberius' appetites, if anything, had been worse. He had purchased Aeliana when she was but a child... and he had no qualms about using her, passing her around among his staff and any visitors who came calling, visitors who shared his perverse desires. As she blossomed into womanhood, ravaged and abused, she found herself on the brink of madness. It was then that she learned of something worse than the abuse she had suffered to that day: She was pregnant.

Carrying the child to term was impossible. The moment Tiberius learned that he or one of his colleagues had planted seed in her, she would be killed. Tiberius would not risk the birth of a bastard, as parentage of such a child would inevitably be attributed to him. She had no idea whose the child might be.

In desperation, she had sought a solution and a way to save her life. She was only barely a woman. She did not know her exact age, but it could not be more than sixteen or seventeen summers. Born a slave, this was the only life she had ever known, but as her hatred for Tiberius grew, so too had her ambition.

She was well liked among Tiberius staff for many reasons, not the least of which was her willingness to use her sex to find favor with the male and female servants alike. The house mistress knew of a Rabbi who might be able to help. She had gone to see this mysterious person, had brought with her every coin she had managed to hoard over the years.

Only when she saw the Rabbi's fangs did she realize she had been tricked. He was not a holy man at all. He was something else. She had heard tales of such creatures — creatures of the night, who killed viciously but who could not themselves be killed. To her surprise, he did not attack.

The Rabbi calmly explained that the house mistress was like him. And if she willed it, he would make her one of them. She would forever be the age she was now; her pregnancy would be terminated; she would not have children for the rest of her unnatural life. Only fire, starvation, or beheading could end her existence. There was, however, a price: She must take blood to live. And once she had become like the Rabbi, she would murder with abandon until her thirst was satisfied.

She had questions. Would she still be able to walk in sunlight? The Rabbi assured her that, yes, she could go about during the day, but sunlight would burn her if she lingered too long. Would she retain her desires as a mortal woman? The Rabbi nodded, laughing, and told her most certainly this was so. Would she possess powers greater than those of mortal men? To an extent, yes, said the Rabbi; she would be stronger and faster.

"Yes," she had told him. "Do it. Please. Do it now."

The Rabbi had leapt, snarling, and she knew a moment's doubt. Had it been a trick? Then his fangs were in her throat. It went on for what seemed like forever... and then his blood was in her mouth, fed to her from a tear he made with his teeth in his own wrist...

When she had awoken in a Roman alleyway, she had been possessed of a thirst, a *need*, to take the blood of those around her. All night she hunted, drinking deeply from whomever she encountered. It had been a glorious night of slaughter, a night of power, a night in which her newfound strength, growing with each victim, spurred her to ever-greater heights of savagery. And then she had realized.

Tiberius.

She could make him *pay*.

From that moment, still his consort, she had worked to destroy him from within, cultivating relationships with Caligula, with Macro, with anyone else she thought might work with her to seize power. Her first act was to find the house mistress and murder her so that her secret would remain intact. Some weeks later, she hunted down the Rabbi and eliminated him, too. Then she turned her full attention to the Emperor.

Her goal was not merely to unseat Tiberius, not merely to take revenge on him for his cruelty to her over the years. It was to see Rome itself fall and burn. She would bring it about if it took centuries... and now she had the centuries in which to do it.

As Caligula thrust into her, as he took his filthy pleasure with her as so many had before him, she pictured how satisfying it would be to reveal her fangs and rip out his throat. She longed to feel his blood soaking her chest, ached to hear the death rattle of his last breath in his lungs. How glorious it would be to feel the reflected heat of Rome put to the torch, as everyone and everything in the city, in the Empire, turned to ash and ascended to the heavens.

She would make it happen. She would show them all. She would one day be more powerful than Tiberius himself... and anyone who touched her without her permission, from this day until eternity, would die in agony.

As Caligula mounted her, she laughed, and continued laughing, until even Caligula wondered what was wrong with her.

"Aeliana?" he said, looming over her, inside her. "Aeliana? Aeliana? Elizabeth? Elizabeth?"

* * *

"Elizabeth? Elizabeth?"

Elizabeth Hawkins' eyes shot open. Caspian had his hand on her shoulder and was trying to rouse her.

"I'm awake, damn it," she said. Her tone was harsher than it needed to be. She hated dreaming of her life *before*.

"We're here," said Caspian. His apology was written in his eyes. In that moment, Hawkins realized that he truly cared for her. He was a loyal soldier, who had stayed with her for many years. He did not deserve to bear the brunt of her displeasure over things that could not change."

"I... apologize, Caspian," she said. The uncharacteristic gesture caused Caspian's eyes to widen. Shaking it off, he handed her his phone.

"A message from our informants in Florida," he said. "Ibn al Farir, Brasov's most trusted lieutenant, was sighted on the hospital grounds. He is there, and if al Farir is there, it means whatever Brasov is protecting is very important indeed."

"That monster," she said, shaking her head. "I don't look forward to en-countering him again."

"There is more," Caspian told her. "The Resistance has hit an armory not far from Brasov's hospital site. It's only a matter of time before they attack. If Brasov truly does have Adam... he may kill Adam to prevent the prize from falling into Resistance hands."

She swore under her breath. "I guarantee Vlad has anticipated this," she said. "He'll know we don't have the manpower to establish dominance for our kind under our banner. And the Resistance, even if Harden's Cousinry backs them openly, does not have the resolve needed to win." She swore again, an ancient curse. In English, she said, "Damn him. He knows. He knows we have to ally with Harden if we wish to beat him. He'll be counting on it. And we've no choice but to trip his trap and try to fight through it."

"Driving you into the arms of an enemy hardly seems like a shrewd ma-neuver," said Caspian.

"You have to understand how Vlad sees women," said Hawkins. "And es-pecially how he sees me. You said it yourself, Caspian, the night he betrayed us. He knows I cannot be controlled. Likely he hopes my inability to work and play well with others will cause friction within the Resistance. They must be completely united if they are to destroy him, and he knows it."

Caspian considered that. "Then what will you do?"

Hawkins sighed. "I will do the one thing he does not expect," she said. "I will deal in good faith with the Resistance." She stepped out of the car. "First, however, there is a loose end that requires attention."

He walked with her through the junkyard. All around them, crushed vehicles, some of them flattened, others crushed into large cubes, were stacked in maze-like columns and rows. There were many such junkyards in the United States. Brasov had not yet made antique automobiles illegal, but she knew this was one of his eventual goals. As it was, there were heavy taxes and fines for owning vehicles that predated smart-cars. All such vehicles were subject to tax stamps for "emissions overages," while very generous tax credits could be had for submitting a voucher certifying that one's obsolete, high-pollution automobile had been destroyed. There were plenty of abuses of the system, as there always were in such systems, but the programs remained in place. As crushingly high as taxes were these days, many people took advantage of the option.

It was a beautiful night. Hawkins drank in the night air, feeling the need to hunt something for dinner. Yes. She would do just that, then take Caspian to her bed. He deserved it and she needed it.

"You're certain?" said Caspian, interrupting her reverie. "He was a faithful servant for many years."

"Faithful, yes," said Hawkins. "Successful, no. His failure is so complete that it cannot go unpunished. You trust your men?"

"Yes."

"Be certain, Caspian, or eliminate them when we are finished."

"I am certain," he said, bristling slightly. "They are my most trusted operatives for that reason. They are loyal to you, Elizabeth."

She nodded.

They reached the massive industrial compactor at the center of the lot. The hydraulic maw of the machine was open. Strapped into the driver seat of an ancient Chevrolet Caprice, which was itself positioned inside the compactor, was Arturo. His hands and feet were bound with fine, high-tensile wire. At full strength, a vampire who was willing to sever his hands and feet could break such a wire. Arturo was far from that strong; had not fed since he was discovered, wounded and humiliated, wandering around outside the ruins of the Simpson estate.

Hawkins had lied to Harden when he taunted her about Arturo's whereabouts. She had been sorely put out when he was finally found after Harden's escape, a bullet still working its way out of his brain. The disorientation he had experienced was normal for a vampire shot directly through the head. The brain healed, but the victim often suffered short-term memory loss. So it had been with Arturo. Evidently he had battled with Harden and lost. The wound, if the powder marks were any indication, had traveled beneath his chin and through his jaw through his skull. That was consistent with close-quarters combat. The bullet was a nine-millimeter slug, probably from Arturo's own MAC-11.

His failure was total. She leaned in through the open window of the driver's side. Arturo stared up at her, his expression bleak. Her men had beaten him and, because he had not fed, he was not healing quickly. His face was puffy and sallow. One of his eyes was swollen shut. There were two guards here — Caspian's men — and they snapped to attention in Hawkins' presence. She signaled to Caspian, who snapped his fingers and pointed. The guards made themselves scarce. Caspian looked to Hawkins and she nodded to him, too. He disappeared into the darkened junkyard.

"Elizabeth..." Arturo said softly. His voice rasped in his throat. "Please..."

"Do you know why I am so angry with you, Arturo?" she asked him. Waiting for a reply that did not come, she finally said, "No? Then I'll tell you. It's the waste. For *years* you shadowed Thomas Simpson... and for *years*, because of your failure, because you somehow tipped your hand, Simpson made fools of us all. There's no telling how much damage your misinformation, tailored to Simpson's benefit, did to my organization. How could you do this to me, Arturo? To *us*? Don't you realize what this means? It means that for years, we were playing directly into the Cousinry's hands. I know you thought you were serving me, Arturo, but this magnitude of betrayal, however unintentional... there is no penalty great enough."

"Please," said Arturo. "Please..."

"Don't," she told him. "Don't make your last works to me begging for your life. Take your punishment, Arturo. Take your *damnation*." She stepped away and walked to the control console for the compactor. Turning, she look at her failed operative one last time. The heavy switch that controlled the machine was protected by a Lexan cover. She opened it.

"Elizabeth!" Arturo hissed. "ELIZABETH!"

Hawkins sighed. A disappointment to his last breath. She pressed her palm down on the compactor switch.

Arturo's screams grew louder and more urgent as the pneumatic arms hummed and whined. The massive arms of the compactor began to crush the Chevrolet. It was a slow, inexorable process. Arturo, in a final act of desperation, managed to sever one of his own hands trying to free himself from the wire — but the bloody stump with which he tried to open the driver's door was useless to him. Finally, eventually, the caprice was flattened and pulled into the innards of the compactor, to be further compressed.

Arturo had stopped screaming by then.

She was consigning him to the worst fate imaginable, for their kind. Some part of him would remain aware of what was happening until the fibers of his being eventually turned to dust from lack of nourishment It would take quite some time, even as weak as Arturo had been. He was lucky, really; if there had been a way to ensure he would suffer forever, without some elaborate scheme revolving around healing him periodically, she might have done so. As it was, she did not have the time for a revenge that elaborate. This would do. It would do nicely.

She did not wait to see the final cube of the Chevrolet emerge from the machine.

Chapter Fifteen

North Chicago, February 14, 1929

Flanking Altan bin Ramseur, Ibn al Farir held his Thompson subma-chinegun at the waist and sprayed the contents of his hundred-round drum throughout the room. The heavy slugs punctured men and furniture alike, splintering wood and shattering bone. Vlad Tepes' human sycophants collapsed in bloody heaps, some of them moaning for help or for a quick death. Al Farir would provide them the latter at the point of the *jambiya* in his belt. The curved blade had been his companion for many years, including when he rode with Altan bin Ramseur against Dracula's forces the *first* time. For their hunt to have come to this, for it to end in a garage in Lincoln Park, amused him. How far they had come, how many thousands on thousands of miles they had trod, for it to come to this.

Vlad Tepes had but one vampire bodyguard, who leapt forward to protect the ancient infidel. Al Farir was more than up to this task. While bin Ramseur dealt with Dracula himself, al Farir concentrated on Vlad Tepes' guard.

From within his tailored suit, the bodyguard produced a katar, a long cut-ting and thrusting blade held in the fist and designed for punching strikes. The bodyguard was slow, however brave he might be. Al Farir brought his knife up and under the man's rib cage, cutting deeply, intending to drive the blade up, over the vampire's chest and into his throat—

The bodyguard slashed with the katar, the tines of the weapon's parallel guard battering the jambiya. The jambiya broke at the hilt, the ancient blade cracking neatly in half at the base. Al Farir roared his displeasure and sunk his teeth into the bodyguard's neck. Once he had ripped out the other vampire's throat, he forced the vampire to the ground and, with the bodyguard's own katar, slowly sawed off his foe's head.

"*Allāhu Akbar!*" he shouted. Turning, still holding the enemy's katar, he was just in time to witness Vlad Tepes' final moments. Altan bin Ramseur had wasted no time on noble gestures or grand battles. His revenge was pragmatic. He had simply emptied his Thompson into Vlad Tepes' face and, when the Impaler fell, he had used the meat cleaver he carried to hack away Vlad Tepes' arms and legs. Another drum of a hundred rounds of .45 ACP had been dumped into the Wallachian's chest. The combined effect left Dracula helpless before bin Ramseur, although he was healing quickly enough to be coherent and capable of speech. The buds of new arms and legs began to form from the bloody stumps of his body. His limbs would not be restored quickly enough for that to matter.

"You thought to punish me," said bin Ramseur, standing over Vlad Tepes with the bloody cleaver still in hand. "You wished to give me the hell that is not death, but life. Yet here I am, infidel. Here I am, powerful, eternal. Your time has finally ended. I will take from you what you, in your arrogance, were too stupid to take from me."

"I am Dracula," Vlad Tepes managed.

"No," said Altan bin Ramseur, raising the cleaver. "*I* am Dracula."

The cleaver fell.

And rose.

And fell again, over and over.

* * *

Florida

The portable monitor had been placed near Adam's head. It contained a fiber-optic camera and microphone pickup. With great difficulty, Adam managed to turn his head toward it. He was no longer healing. He had gone too long without blood.

Brasov's face was still on the monitor. He had watched Adam for what seemed like hours, sitting in silence. Adam recognized the setting from the background. Brasov sat in the Oval Office, his fingers steepled, his expression grim. But Adam no longer cared.

"You disappoint me," said Brasov, giving voice to Adam's own thoughts. When my operatives stumbled across you in Lhasa, when they told me that the vampires of Tibet whispered your name as *Gyed*, I knew I had finally found Adam. The first vampire, long whispered among our kind to exist somewhere in the world. A creature as old as time itself. Gyed is 'eight' in Tibetan. The symbol for infinity. It was said you were so old that there was nothing you did not know. That the Tibetans considered you a *tulpa*, a mystic holy man. It was my hope that by bringing you in, by imprisoning you here, by guarding you closely until I had pried from you the secrets of vampire immortality, I would be ensuring the future of vampires everywhere. You could have been a part of that, Adam. You could have had an honored place in my regime. Global Sharia is coming. I shall be the world's first vampire caliph. Under my rule, order will reign. The people of Allah will prosper. And the infidels will be exterminated once and for all."

"I... am curious..." whispered Adam through his chapped lips.

"Yes?" said Brasov, leaning forward on the monitor.

"Why... did you take... Vlad Tepes' name?"

"You knew him," said Brasov. "Of course. You have known many of the world's famous vampires, have you not? Perhaps all of them. One as old as you... there is no telling what information might lie within your mind."

"There... must be more," said Adam. "Was it... only power? You must have felt... a kinship... to vampires. You picked... a symbol... that would inspire."

"I picked a symbol that was politically expedient," said Brasov. "There are no ideals, Adam. There are only expediencies." Brasov sighed. "I am going to instruct Ibn al Farir to continue torturing you. You will eventually die at his hands, yes. But before you do, he will learn whatever secrets there are left inside your stubborn skull. You can ease your way by telling him as much as you do remember. I suppose I shall have to accept that you have lived so long that you truly can tell me nothing of your beginnings." Brasov shook his head. "Such a waste. Such a terrible waste. Good-bye, Adam. We will not speak again. I have more important things to do."

The monitor went dark.

Adam stared at the ceiling. The thought of the hours, days, even weeks of torment that might still remain might have terrified him centuries past. Now, however, he did not care. It did not matter. Nothing mattered.

All that mattered was that his will had held. It would have to be enough. He would have to continue to resist until al Farir finally managed to kill him. It was the only way. Al Farir was a monster... but there were so many like him and Brasov. There were so many soulless predators among Adam's many descendants. It was this, more than anything else, that broke his heart.

Vampires like Brasov must never know the truth.

They must never learn how vampires came to be.

* * *

Ibn al Farir stepped into the hallway, stripped to the waist, wearing his pistol belt and his knife. He had managed to pick up an AK100 from the locker in his temporary quarters. Extra thirty-round magazines were thrust into his waistband. He was a powerful, fearsome figure as he stalked the corridor of the hospital. Red lights strobed as the facility alarm continued to hoot with maddeningly arrhythmic timing. The alarm was old, something that had been installed with the founding of the hospital. Brasov's men had not thought to replace it, so now he must fight with the sound of a giant, dying goose bleating in his ears.

No matter. He hurried to the security room, where display screens covered the walls and the cameras watching over the facility could be monitored from a single desk. One of Brasov's human devotees, a simpering whelp named Evan, looked up from his post as al Farir strode in.

"Report," said the vampire.

Evan pointed, apparently having difficulty finding the necessary words. Three of the twelve screens had gone dark, their pictures returning nothing but blue "no input" displays. Movement in one of the remaining displays caught al Farir's eye. As he watched, a man in camouflage fatigues, carrying another AK100, shot out the camera.

"They are targeting surveillance to clear the way for a frontal assault," said Farir. "The fools. This is precisely what the facilities ground defenses are arranged to prevent." Farir had seen to the placement of the mixed human and Fedvamp security forces himself. There were barricades in every stairwell of the hospital, sandbag gun emplacements on the roof, and trucks parked at strategic intervals on the asphalt ribbons leading to the old hospital building itself. The trucks would prevent anyone from driving a vehicle close to the hospital; they served as mobile bollards. Al Farir was well experienced in warfare and confident in his preparations. Whatever suicidal impulse had prompted the Resistance to strike this facility would result in only their doom.

Several more of the screens went dark. It was only a matter of time before the Resistance scouts got them all. Farir dismissed it as a lost cause. It would not be enough for the infidels to claim victory.

"Sir," said Evan. "The perimeter security alarms have been tripped."

Al Farir frowned. Several LEDs were now blinking on Evan's control console. The outer perimeter was guarded by a buried piezoelectric line that could be triggered only by heavy machinery. That meant the Resistance were indeed bringing in vehicles. Were it Al Farir, he would want to bring troop trucks close, following the scouts. The scouts eliminated the cameras, blinding security operations within the hospital. But there would be no way for them to get past the trucks. He was certain of it.

An explosion rocked the hospital.

It was followed by another, and another. Al Farir's sensitive hearing picked up the sound of the incoming round just before another blast, closer this time, shattered windows in adjacent rooms.

Mortars.

It was impossible to prevent the Resistance forces from getting small arms. Most of Brasov's interdiction efforts were therefore focused on the types of munitions that could do serious harm to armored equipment and to facilities. If the Resistance had access to mortars, his defenses might well be inadequate. In fact, if an even moderately competent tactician were to consider the risks, they might well decide to—

A force that felt like the hand of Allah pressed him into the floor. It was heat and pressure and sound so deafening that he feared, for a moment, that he had gone deaf. One moment Evan had been there, crouched over his largely useless security console. The next minute, he was red vapor and chunks of meat, while Al Farir himself was pinned to the floor under a mountain of debris. The rushing of his own blood within his skull was soon replaced by a ringing noise. Above him, he could see the blue of the morning sky. The air was filled with smoke and the stench of human flesh.

It took him a moment to process what had happened. The rebels. The Resistance had fired a mortar shell at the building. It had struck the corner nearest the security office. It had very nearly killed him.

He had lost his rifle in the explosion. No matter. He had his pistol and his kerambit. Snarling, he shoved the wreckage from his body. His body healed as he strode into the corridor, determined to find and destroy these enemies who dared threaten Brasov's will.

Another explosion rocked the building, and then another. The Resistance was shelling the far side of the structure, walking their rounds across the periphery of the building. That was logical. The security office sat at one corner and was a clear target. But if the Resistance were here, if they were assaulting this facility, there could be only one reason. They wished to know what Brasov was protecting here in Florida — or, perhaps worse, they suspected that Adam, the world's oldest vampire, was held captive here.

Resistance spies were everywhere. Al Farir would have to stand before his leader and admit his role in this tactical failure, for it had been Ibn al Farir who urged the scaling up of security around the hospital. No doubt the sheer size of the force here had been enough to alert the enemy to Adam's presence. But it was al Farir's firm belief that, in war, no secret could be kept forever. Better to have the resources in place to fight back the enemy than to trust to secrecy and subterfuge to keep their prize under wraps.

But that was another failure al Farir would have to answer for. The interrogation of Adam had revealed nothing so far. It had become an obsession, of sorts, for al Farir; he wanted to break Adam, not simply to please Brasov or to serve Brasov's cause... but because Adam continued to defy him. The vampire claimed, again and again, that he was too old to remember. That he had lived so long that his own genesis escaped him, was forgotten.

Al Farir did not believe it.

He would break the prisoner. He would take the information Brasov wanted. He would succeed.

But first, these impudent whelps must be put down.

He had killed many Resistance fighters through the years. Their attacks were growing more brazen, which al Farir believed was a sign of desperation. That was good. The tighter Brasov closed his fist, the more they squirmed, and the bolder they became. Once emboldened, they finally revealed themselves, allowing al Farir, the Fedvamps, and the Basij to stamp them out.

As he approached the stairwell, the building shook yet again. The bell of a fire alarm finally sounded, somewhere in the depths of the old hospital. There were sprinkler heads built into the ceilings, but these had been deactivated years before. The teams sent to ready the building prior to Adam's internment there had seen no need to reactivate those systems. Al Farir realized, now, that this was a serious oversight. Fire was one of the few true enemies of a vampire. It seemed impossible, now, that he might have overlooked this.

Gunfire echoed up the stairs. Al Farir pushed open the fire door, Stetchkin pistol in hand, and risked sticking his head out to peer down to the floors below. A rattle of Kalashnikov fire drove him back. Bullets struck the cinderblock walls above and behind him.

"Infidels!" al Farir roared. "Face me, cowards!"

The enemy gunfire stopped. A voice echoed from below. "Hey!" it said. "Hey, vampire!"

"I am Ibn al Farir, lieutenant to Woodrow Brasov!" he bellowed back. "You will fall before me!"

"Just one thing," said the voice.

"You are the coward!" said Farir. He leaned farther out, daring them to shoot at him once more. He saw the face of a man far below. "Are you human, or a vampire traitor? Name yourself to me, so that I may know whom I slay!"

"My name is Vincent Harden," shouted the man at bottom of the stairs. "I'm the leader of the Cousinry. This man next to me is Van Gogh. He's the leader of the Resistance. And this thing he's holding is one of your government's rocket-propelled grenade launchers."

Ibn al Farir's eyes widened.

The rocket-propelled grenade streaked up the stairwell on a plume of smoke. It was fast, but not *that* fast; it did not accelerate as a bullet did.

It was faster than a vampire, though.

Chapter Sixteen

Harden's leg had begun to ache. He had kicked in every door on that floor. But at last, at long last, he found the interrogation room he sought. There was a vampire inside strapped to a gurney. The smells that hit Harden's nose, once inside the chamber of horrors, were vile... and familiar. Beneath the smell of blood, behind the smells of human misery, was something else. It was the same smell he had sensed in Thomas Simpson's home as the vampire starved himself to death.

He thought perhaps the vampire on the gurney was already dead. At Harden's approach, the prisoner's eyes opened. They were filmy, the pupils dilated. He had seen that before. It was common in vampires who had not fed for so long that death was near.

"Are you Adam?" Harden said softly.

The vampire looked from him to Tag, who was guarding the doorway with her Thompson. "Yes," he whispered. His voice was almost gone.

"We're here to rescue you," said Harden. "We're going to free you."

"It doesn't matter," whispered Adam.

"Will you come with us?" Harden asked.

"Very... well," said Adam. He waited, resigned, as Harden disconnected the steel cables, which were hooked underneath the gurney. He even appeared to try to move. He could not do much more than raise his head off the bedding.

"I'll help you," said Harden. He got his arm under Adam, who felt incredibly fragile. With some difficulty, he managed to get Adam standing again. Half-dragging, half-carrying the ancient vampire, Harden turned and gestured to Tag. "We've got to go."

"Harden," she said, frowning. She had her radio in her hand; a wireless, bone-transducing earpiece for it was clipped behind her ear. "Reinforcements. Fedvamps and Basij, moving in from all sides, according to our lookouts."

"As we figured," said Harden. He'd anticipated that; there would be more troops staged far enough away to avoid attack, but close enough to bolster the hospital's troops, if the facilitate came under attack. It was why he had structured the raid as he had, why he had relied on a ground blitz to bring troop trucks through the perimeter while their forces shelled the building. "Signal the perimeter forces to retreat. We'll meet Van Gogh on the roof."

"Do you think he can handle this al Farir character?"

"He's smart enough to hold back, keep the vampire trapped on the roof, if he can't," said Harden. "But we'll need to clear the way for our exfiltration. Signal Blackbird One and Blackbird Two. It's time."

Exfiltration had to be precisely timed. The reinforcements would likely have anti-air weapons. If Harden, Tag, Van Gogh, and their rescued vampire were not in the air fast, they were not going to get far.

"Come on," said Harden to Adam. "We're getting you out of here."

* * *

Ibn al Farir burst through the fire door from the access stairs and onto the roof. Fires burned here and there. Smoking craters marked it in several places where the mortar shells had done their business. Any personnel he might have had stationed on the roof were gone, either killed or fled under the shelling. There was still sporadic gunfire from the hospital below.

He had to get control of the situation, had to marshal his forces. Adam would wait until...

No. *No!* He had taken too much damage to the brain. He had forgotten what he had been about to do. He had to take Adam's life, deny him to the Resistance. It was the only act Brasov would accept. If Adam fell into the hands of the Cousinry... the damage done could be incalculable. Ibn al Farir's own life would be forfeit.

His jaw and tongue were still healing, which made his speech sound slurred as he shouted into the radio. He roared to make himself heard.

"All units! Move in now! Gunships to my location!"

The voice on the other end of the radio told him it would be several minutes. This only enraged him further. His flesh was scorched black, his wounds still knitting together. The pain was excruciating. He had lost his pistol in the blast.

He heard the helicopters before he saw them. The two Boeing craft came in low and slow, level with the roof of the hospital, skimming over the tree line in what al Farir assumed was a bid to avoid federal radar sweeps.

The fire door slammed open again. Al Farir turned and caught a bullet in the hand. He dropped his radio. His lip curling in a bloodthirsty sneer, he drew his kerambit knife and spun it by the ring, dropping into a low crouch.

The Resistance came boiling through the doorway. The one called Van Gogh was leading. But there, too, was Harden, carrying the decrepit Adam under one arm. There was a woman, too, a very lovely woman. Ibn al Farir promised himself he would rape the infidel whore on the corpses of the others before draining her dry.

"Blackbird One, Blackbird Two," said Van Gogh into his own radio. "Begin your descent—"

One of the helicopters exploded.

* * *

"Anti-air!" shouted Harden. He gestured to Tag, who took Adam from him, propping him up with his arm over her shoulder. Van Gogh and his men ran to the edge of the roof and began firing with their rocket-propelled grenade launchers. Explosions began to shake the ground below the hospital. Their targets were a skirmish line of Federal troops moving toward the hospital. The counter-fire prevented another anti-air missile from being launched, but there was no telling how long they could suppress another launch.

"Go!" shouted Van Gogh in his strange accent. "Get to the chopper! We will hold them while you escape!"

"No," said Ibn al Farir. "You will have to face me first. And know that I have this." He held up the plastic square of a remote detonator. To Harden, he said, "*You* know what this is."

"I'll fight you," said Harden, nodding.

"I will kill every last one of you. None of you will leave this rooftop alive." His eyes met Tag's. "And *you* will suffer in ways you have never thought possible, before I take your life while inside you."

"Vincent, what are you *doing*?" demanded Tag.

"He'll rip the chopper apart if we don't end him before it lands," said Harden.

"Then *shoot* him!" Tag shouted. She struggled to bring up her Thompson.

"He's holding a detonator," said Harden. "I can smell it, Tag. I can smell it all over this roof. A human being couldn't, but I can. It smells like almonds."

"Semtex," said Tag softly. "We can hit him before he pushes it!"

"The entire building is wired to explode," said al Farir, smiling. He held the detonator with his left hand, his thumb over the button. "I *guarantee* I can press it, even if you take my head."

Harden stepped forward. He took the Special Forces tomahawk from his belt.

"Harden, no!" shouted Tag.

"So like an infidel," said al Farir. He crept closer, spinning his kerambit by its ring, moving the curved blade in intricate patterns through the air. "Leashed by your woman. Does she give you permission to mount her, too? Does she tell you when you may speak?"

Harden ignored his words. It was so much noise. You never let an enemy engage you in dialogue in a fight. You never let him get you thinking about an answer. You let his words wash over you, ignored, as you looked for an opening...

Al Farir lunged. His blade cut through the air. Harden hit back, hacking with the Tomahawk. He used it first to slash al Farir's arm, then break it. Hooking the arm, he passed it through and then rammed the point of the tomahawk into the vampire's ribs. Al Farir grunted and stumbled. His kerambit remained where it was, held fast with this index finger through the ring. His broken arm popped as the bone knitted and straightened.

"You fight well, infidel," said al Farir.

Again Harden ignored him. This seemed to enrage al Farir, who renewed his attack. He slashed and lunged, moving in and out in the space between the two vampires, his footwork excellent and his footing sure. Harden had fought others as good as al Farir, but not many. This was a warrior as adept at combat as Harden himself.

Another streak of smoke flashed through the sky above them. The remaining helicopter, which had been circling the building while waiting for the landing zone to clear, was almost hit. The pilot managed to avoid the rocket at the last possible moment.

They were running out of time. He had to end this.

He dropped his guard, opening himself up to a deadly cut. Then he shifted his stance, putting himself on al Farir's left. The vampire would shift to compensate.

Al Farir was clearly adept at Silat or something very like it, one of many blade-aware martial arts originating in the Muslim world. Like any trained warrior, he had his habits. He had his ingrained muscle memory. Move a certain way, and the left hand, the hand holding the detonator, would move to check and clear without conscious thought.

There!

Harden hacked with the tomahawk. He severed al Farir's left hand at the wrist. Both the hand and the detonator fell away. The vampire opened his mouth to scream in pain, but Harden was faster. He buried his tomahawk in al Farir's skull, splitting it open and pushing the point of the tomahawk deep into al Farir's brain.

The vampire fell to the tar roof of the hospital, twitching. Harden moved in to finish him, to remove his head if he had to hack it away piece by piece.

The helicopter dodged another rocket. This one was even closer. They were simply out of time.

"Go, go, go," Van Gogh was shouting now. He signaled the helicopter to land. A cyclone of ash and debris was whipped up as the chopper touched down. Reluctantly, Harden left the immobilized al Farir and ran to Tag. Between the two of them, they managed to hasten Adam to the helicopter. Van Gogh, however, shook his head when they gestured for him to follow.

"Come on!" shouted Tag. "We've got to go!"

"I will stay to cover your retreat," he said. "It is the only way you will survive." His men kept up a furious rate of fire, blowing through the ammunition for their rifles while firing RPGs as if they were going out of style. The explosions below sounded like Fourth of July fireworks — or what those fireworks had sounded like before Brasov's administration banned these for being potentially offensive to Muslims and minority groups.

"Do you realize what you're doing?" Harden said to him. "Van Gogh, it's suicide!"

Van Gogh leaned in so that only Harden could hear him. "I was never the leader the Resistance needs," he said. "With you helping us, Vincent, we have done more in days than I have managed in years. Take command of the Resistance, Mister Harden. Take command and free our country from Brasov and his evil. If I lose my life here, it is the least I can give for the dream that we will one day be free again."

Harden started to protest. "But you can still—"

"Please," said Van Gogh. "Let me have this."

Harden nodded. Jaw tight, he put his hand on Van Gogh's shoulder, clasping it firmly, before turning and dragging Adam to the chopper with Tag. He thought he saw tears streaming down Tag's face as they piled into the helicopter. The moment the last of Van Gogh's team were aboard, they were taking off again.

From the air, the battle looked grim, the hospital worse. The fires were spreading. Van Gogh's people had pulled out just in time. A cordon of federal troops was now surrounding the building. They had MRAP trucks and even an old Abrams tank. The tanks were obsolete, but Brasov had deployed many of them for domestic "peacekeeping." Others were being used overseas, where they grossly overmatched by the Muslim armored units they faced.

Van Gogh and the soldiers who had opted to stay behind with him continued to trade fire with the advancing federals. As the roof of the hospital faded from view, Harden could see Ibn al Farir up and moving again. The thought of the evil vampire living through this battle left a knot in his gut. His mind raced with the many possibilities, the things he *could* have done, the things he *might* have done.

That was it, then, wasn't it? That was why he had avoided joining the fight for so long. It wasn't fighting that Harden feared. It wasn't battle. He had lived through countless wars. He had fought countless enemies. What worried him, though, was the thought of making mistakes. The idea that others would die because of decisions he made. The thought of that responsibility, that *weight*, terrified him.

"There is... a broadcast station... in Tampa," said Adam. "You need... to get me there... while there is time."

Harden reached back and touched his pack, as if to reassure himself that it was still there. He nodded.

Tag reached across Adam's seat to put her hand on Harden's. She looked into his eyes as if to reassure him, to tell him they were going to be okay. He needed that right now. He nodded to her. She inclined her chin toward the cockpit of the helicopter.

The pilot was shouting something even Harden could not hear from the cockpit. He was gesturing wildly, enough to have caught Tag's attention.

"What?" said Harden.

The pilot pointed to the intercom headsets in a rack on the crew seats. Harden took one and put it on.

"I said, strap in," said the pilot. "We're going to have to duck and weave to avoid any more surface-to-air rockets if they follow us on the ground. I can't tell if they're shadowing us or not, but I don't dare gain altitude or federal radar will paint us. Who's senior now? I need to know where we're going."

"Who's what?" said Tag. She had also donned a headset. In the seat between her and Harden, Adam slouched with his eyes closed. The vampire was still alive — Harden would have been able to sense that even if he hadn't spoken — but he was very weak. He was so like Thomas had been at the end.

"Who's *senior*," said the Resistance pilot. "I need orders. Who's in charge?"

Harden and Tag exchanged glances.

"I think..." Harden said, pausing. "I think *I* am."

Chapter Seventeen

Ibn al Farir was mad with bloodlust. He fought his way through the Resistance fighters with his bare hands, ripping them limb from limb, feeding in brief gulps as he tore through them. They were nothing to him; they were infidels; they were mere human beings. They would not live to see another dawn.

Their bullets tore into him. He caught dozens of slugs in the chest, in the arms, in his legs. He felt his neck being punctured and briefly crouched, huddling, making sure he did not lose his head. A bullet grazed the top of his skull but did not penetrate his brain. He was furious. He had never known such rage.

The wreckage of the first of the two Resistance helicopters burned on the grounds next to the hospital, but the other craft had escaped. More of the Resistance fighters had fled, their retreat covered by the squad of men led by this Van Gogh. The name was familiar to Ibn al Farir. For many years, Van Gogh had led the Resistance against Brasov. He had never before managed a raid of this size and scope, never achieved a success of this nature.

Brasov would be furious, too.

The Resistance fighters were falling back. He chased them, ripping at the soldiers closest to the rear, pulling off arms and legs and tearing bloody chunks from their flanks. They tried to scramble down the stairwell, to escape him, to go anywhere that he could not reach, but it was too late for them. He followed them down, harrying them the entire way, killing one after another. They were not prepared to fight a vampire. They were only human.

There was but one left when they finally reached the ground floor of the burning hospital. It was the one called Van Gogh. He had suffered serious wounds. His chest was soaked with blood and he could barely stand. Onward he limped, trying to escape his fate. Ibn al Farir drew his folding kerambit, spinning it without thinking about the motion. His left hand had long since grown back, its growth spurred by blood he had drained from the Resistance men.

Al Farir caught up to Van Gogh easily. As the human tried to limp away, al Farir slashed the back of Van Gogh's legs with the kerambit. The Resistance leader shrieked and fell. Al Farir used the toe of his boot to roll the pathetic mortal onto his back. Then the vampire put his foot in Van Gogh's chest.

"Do you have any last words before he crush your skull, infidel?" said Ibn al Farir.

"Just... that you... dropped this," gasped Van Gogh.

In his hand was Ibn al Farir's lost detonator.

Van Gogh pressed the button.

The explosion seared Ibn al Farir's eyes and blew him into the tree line.

* * *

Harden's ears pricked up. "Did you... Did you hear that?"

"Hear what?" asked Tag.

"We're getting reports the hospital has gone up," reported the pilot.

"Van Gogh?" asked Harden.

"No, sir," said the pilot. "No word. I'm sorry, sir. Van Gogh was a good man."

Harden hung his head. Tag put her hand on his shoulder.

"What's your name?" she asked the pilot.

"Everyone calls me Remy," said the pilot. "Sydney Remington Carver, at your service."

"How much fuel do we have left, Remy?" asked Harden. He couldn't let himself mourn Van Gogh now. There was too much work to do.

"I can get us to the fallback base, Mountain Two," said Remy.

"No," said Harden. "That's not what we need." He took stock of the armed men and women in the chopper with them. The Boeing was a big chopper, a twin-rotor troop-mover. They had enough people. "Are you carrying any ammo?"

"Some, sir," said Remy.

"Everybody!" said Harden, waving his arms to get the attention of any Resistance people who weren't wearing headsets. "Listen up. Do an ammo check and load up on whatever you can. Bring your packs. We're going to land and acquire transportation, then break up and move overland back to Mountain Two when we've completed our mission."

"Mission?" asked Tag.

Harden looked at Adam, who had passed out. "We need to get him in front of a television camera. Something with a wide coverage area."

"There's a little independent Christian outfit outside Tampa," said Remy. "Brasov banned Christian over-air programming, but they've been running to protest the law for a couple of months now."

"Too small," said Harden. "I need a blowtorch station, something that can reach most of the state. They're going to shut us down the minute they can manage it. We need to reach as many people as we can, initially, so the video will reach people who can record it and upload it to the etherways. We need to go viral."

"What are we broadcasting?" asked Tag.

Harden inclined his chin to Adam. "Not us. Him."

"WBSV in Tampa," said Remy. "They broadcast in digital high definition to all of Florida. But it's state-controlled. There will be Fedvamps and human federal troops in place. It'd take an Army to hold the joint for long enough to broadcast."

"Then it's just our luck," said Harden, looking at the Resistance soldiers, "that we have one."

* * *

Basij Temple Headquarters, Tampa

Aibir Faisal, Tampa's Deputy Caliph, pressed his forehead to the prayer mat, bowing low in obeisance to Allah. The loudspeakers built into the minarets of the building blared the Call to Prayer throughout the residential neighborhood. That had been a problem in the earliest days of the temple, when it had been merely a mosque and not the district headquarters for the Tampa enclave's Muslim militia. The foolish infidels had even tried to go to court to silence the Call, arguing that this was interfering with the peaceful enjoyment of their homes. Truly, the Westerners' Islamaphobia knew no bounds. It was why, in the first years of the twenty-first century, they had resisted the waves of thousands of Muslim colonists coming to the United States to start new lives and establish Sharia in the hated West. They were ever a regressive people, after all — slow to embrace the truth, if ever.

Purity sweeps of the enclave had cleared out most of the infidels over the last ten years or so. It was during those years that the role of the Basij had become so integral to Brasov's government. While they were not Fedvamps, the Basij worked hand in hand with the federal vampire troops whenever the government and the Basij's own Imams thought the cooperation productive. There were some who called the Basij the street soldiers of the Fedvamps, doing "dirty work" the government could not be seen, overtly, to be doing. Such was the way of infidels. They were paranoid. They saw potential enemies under every rock and behind every tree.

Fortunately for Faisal and all who followed Allah, the infidels were also weak. They were afraid to be called racist or Islamophobic. They would bend over backward to comply with the demands of groups like the Council for the Defense of Islam and Prevention of Blaspheming Against Islam. It was this, Faisal privately believed, that had made it possible for Woodrow Brasov to take power and then extend his term in office through executive order. After all, he was both a vampire and a vocal supporter of Islamic values. To oppose his policies was to admit that one hated Muslims. How strange that so many in the West seemed to care so deeply what their enemies thought of them — enemies who would gladly slit their throats like the filthy pigs that they were.

The thought of filthy pigs reminded Faisal that he had business to attend to this day. He finished his prayers and stood, hurrying to the recreation room at the rear of the temple. One of his men, Mohammad Sampson, stood guard. Sampson was a black Islamist, a member of the Loin of Islam and a former leader of the Black Supremacist Union. He had proven his worthiness to Faisal many times. Despite the color of his skin, which of course was a handicap for any man, Sampson was capable enough that Faisal had named him Deputy Director of the Tampa Mutaween. The Basij were the Islamic militia, but the Mutaween were responsible for Sharia patrols and purity sweeps — for enforcing the Allah's benevolent, peaceful will on the streets of Tampa.

Sampson opened the door for Faisal and closed it quietly behind the Deputy Caliph. The latch clicked as Sampson locked it. No one would disturb Faisal's much-needed leisure time. He afforded himself precious little of it.

The woman strapped to the cot in the recreation room had been beaten, as was proper. She had already suffered the attentions of several of the Basij, preparing her for this final interlude. Her underwear had been used to gag her, the cloth tied tightly at the back of her neck. Tears streaked her face.

Faisal began to loosen his robes. He had a folding stiletto, a keenly sharp knife that he kept in a pocket sewn into his left sleeve. He would take his pleasure with the infidel girl and then cut her throat. It was the only fate suitable for her. She had been seen in public within the enclave without a head scarf, flaunting her body. This would not do, and if Faisal had to personally rape every infidel who wandered into the enclave, he would do so. He had also instructed the Mutaween to begin extending the range of their patrols beyond the borders of the enclave. Infidels found on the streets exhibiting lewd or drunken behavior, or otherwise offending Allah, would be beaten to punish them for their crimes. The Basij had an arrangement with the Tampa police. There would be no legal reprisals for any such Sharia patrols provided they occurred within walking distance from the enclave.

It was a start. Faisal would slowly increase the range of those patrols. His ultimate goal was to place all of Tampa under Sharia. Only then would he be satisfied... but there would be many whore infidels, like this one, who would have to be taught the beauty and peace of submission to Allah.

The girl began to scream into her gag. Faisal's palms started to sweat. He was going to enjoy this. That was right and good. Allah promised virgins in the afterlife for this very reason. Men should enjoy themselves, and of course there was nothing about an infidel whore that need be respected.

The radio hanging from a lanyard around Faisal's neck began to vibrate. He cursed in frustration, stepped away from the cot, and fished the device from within his robes. Keying it, he hissed, "Yes? What is it?"

"Forgive me, Holy One," said the voice of one of his Mutaween deputies, Mohammad Abja. "We have received a summons on the federal channel. We are to mobilize and await further orders. Resistance forces have staged a terrorist attack on a hospital in Tampa's industrial district."

"What hospital is this?"

"The report does not say, Holy One."

"No matter. Prepare the trucks. Issue the call of highest urgency and assemble the men for patrol."

"Yes, Holy One."

Faisal looked down at the helpless girl. How tempting her whore's body was. It would be a shame to forestall her final lesson in the will of Allah.

"I will join you... shortly," said Faisal, licking his lips.

"Yes, Holy One."

* * *

The guard stationed in the shack at the entrance to the WBSV parking lot had time to look up and open his mouth. Then the shack and the guard exploded.

The guard, like most of the key personnel at WBSV, was one of Brasov's Fedvamps. A thermal check of the grounds, using one of the Resistance soldiers' infrared binoculars, had shown that much. Remy brought the Boeing down fast and hard, fanning the deck with his rotors. The Resistance soldiers piled out with Harden and Tag leading them.

Harden was fully geared up with his pack, his shoulder bag, his full complement of personal weapons, and an AK100 rifle. He also had, strapped to the MOLLE straps of his pack, a heavy-blade machete. Tag had added an identical weapon to her own pack. All of the Resistance fighters carried such blades. They had done battle with the Fedvamps for years, incurring heavy losses in

146

the process. Harden recognized tactics and gear born of long, bitter experience when he saw it. Vietnam had been much the same way.

He shook off the bitter thoughts that Vietnam always brought to mind. That was then. This was now, and now was the time to fight for America in earnest. No more sitting on the sidelines. No more nursing his own wounds, his own tragic memories, while good people fought, suffered, and died.

At the rear of the Resistance group, two soldiers had been detailed to help Adam along. The mysterious and presumably very ancient vampire had been offered blood. Specifically, one of the women within the Resistance's ranks had offered to let him feed from her, provided Harden was on hand to stop Adam from going too far. Even Tag had been reluctant to make an offer like that, and she now had more reason than most to put faith in at least some of vampire kind. But Adam had refused. He simply would not eat.

It's Thomas all over again, Harden thought. *He wants to die. He's had enough and he wants it to end.*

The rebels fanned out and covered the corners of the broadcast station as Harden, in the lead, hit the double doors leading into the facility. At his signal, his support personnel, armed with rotary 40mm grenade launchers — the same weapons that had demolished the guard shack at the edge of the parking lot — took up positions on either side of Harden and Tag. He knew what would be waiting for them. He had asked himself how, if he had an unlimited supply of vampire soldiers at his command, he would choose to protect a state-controlled television station. The rest was tactics, experience, and common sense.

The Fedvamps hiding in the lobby popped up from behind the armored counter that protected them.

"Now," said Harden.

The 40mm grenades chunked from their launchers, one after another. They were HE, or high explosive rounds. The Resistance used HE and beehive rounds alternating in their rotary launchers for a combination of firepower and close-quarters impact. The beehive rounds essentially turned the launcher into a massive shotgun, unleashing with each shot a cluster of ten .22 Long Rifle rounds.

Harden dropped to one knee and shielded his face. Tag and the Resistance fighters hit the deck.

The explosion tore the counter apart, ripping into the Fedvamps and splitting them open. The smoke had not yet cleared when the Resistance fell on the wounded vampires, their machetes hacking and slashing, separating the Fedvamps' heads from their shoulders. It was bloody, grueling work.

"On your nine!" shouted Tag. Harden turned to his nine o'clock to see several uniformed security guards emerge from the corridor that led farther into the broadcast site. He chopped them down with a blast from the MAC-11. There were four, two of whom would not rise again. The other two were Fedvamps. The nine millimeter rounds did not even slow them.

Two of the Resistance grenadiers appeared on either side of Harden. The Cousinry vampire's presence was galvanizing them, giving them both a leader to follow and the impression — largely in error — that they were now undefeatable. Harden wasn't sure how to feel about that.

Beehive rounds ripped the Fedvamps' heads to meaty tatters.

A sign in the corridor pointed to a stairwell labeled "To Booths A/B." That would be the broadcast area. Harden took the lead, stopping when several bullets struck the ceiling near his head. There was a gunman somewhere above, in the stairwell. The gunshots sounded like a small-caliber pistol. Before the Resistance soldiers could look to him to ask what to do, Harden simply walked up the stairs.

A few shots struck him in the chest. He used his arm to shield his face. Another round struck his arm and remained in the flesh until it was pushed out by the healing wound. The bullet clattered to the floor. It was a .25 ACP.

When he reached the top of the stairs, he found himself staring at a single, terrified human in a white, short-sleeve shirt and black tie. The man was middle-aged, his tie at half mast, his hair thinning and disheveled. In his hand he held a Raven MP-25, an ancient handgun that had been banned by Brasov's government along with all inexpensive "Saturday Night Specials." The man's fingers were white on the gun; he was trying to squeeze the trigger, but the little pistol was empty.

"The slide doesn't lock back," said Harden, almost bored. He plucked the gun from the man's hand and dropped it into his bag. Then he grabbed the man by the throat and pushed him against the wall, next to the fire door leading to the broadcast booths.

"Who are you? What do you want?"

Harden looked down at the man's ID badge, which was clipped to his shirt pocket. The badge read, "Alan Cord," and beneath that, "Broadcast Director."

"Funny you should ask that," said Harden, as his armed Resistance fighters started filling up the stairs behind him. "It turns out you're just the person we need to talk to."

"I won't help terrorists!" said Cord. "I won't make trouble!"

"Don't worry," said Harden. "*I'm* the one who's going to make trouble."

Chapter Eighteen

Washington, District of Brasovia

The girl slumped to the carpeted floor of the little access room. Brasov left her where she fell. Wiping his mouth with the back of his hand, he left the little room, emerging into the Oval Office. It was rumored that, years ago, one of the forerunners of the Social Democrats had taken his pleasure with White House interns in that little room. Brasov thought of this often when draining a young woman in that space. It seemed somehow... fitting.

An ashen-faced Orin Weld sat behind the Resolute Desk.

"Orin?" said Brasov. "What are you doing? Why are you sitting in my chair?"

It was then that Brasov realized the transmitter, concealed within the Resolute Desk, had raised itself into position. That only happened when a transmission came in. Direct communiqués from Brasov's field operatives were rare, and to activate the transmitter required one to rotate the placard on the desk. Brasov's placard bore the slogan, "From each according to his ability."

Orin must have entered the office for some business or other and, hearing the beeping of the transmitter, stepped to the desk to investigate. Thereupon he must have fumbled about looking for the source of the noise until he accidentally triggered the device.

"I... I am so sorry, President Brasov," said Weld, on the verge of tears. "I meant no harm. I only wanted to help, but... but..."

"What is it, Orin?"

"Ibn al Farir reports from the field that 'Adam has been lost to the Resistance. He begs your forgiveness and extends his willingness to 'give his life in recompense for his failure.' He says that the Cousinry, led by Vincent Harden, is now directly aiding the Resistance, and it was this that 'turned the tide,' in his words. He... He further states that Adam knows the truth about you, sir. That you are not... not Count Dracula, as so many believe."

Brasov stood, unmoving, for a long moment. "Oh, Orin," he finally said. "I'm so sorry, sir."

Brasov came to stand behind the little man. When Weld made a move to stand, Brasov gently held him in place, his hands on Weld's shoulders.

"No, Orin," said Brasov. "Sit in the chair. Look out at the office. This is what it feels like to be president, Orin. The weight of many decisions rests on you when you see the world from this desk. The chair, while comfortable, is also a burden. And sometimes those decisions, those difficult choices, require you to do things which test your strength. Things that require you to put your goals ahead of your petty whims."

"Yes, sir. I understand, sir."

"Poor Orin," said Brasov. "You realize what I must do?"

"Of... of course, sir. It was a mistake. But I realize... I mustn't... I cannot be allowed to live."

"It isn't that I don't believe in your steadfast loyalty, Orin," said Brasov. "Even given what you have just learned. It is that I cannot have any mere human knowing things that could be tortured from him. You are a liability to me, Orin. You understand this?"

"I do, sir. I'm sorry, sir."

"So you are," said Brasov. His hands caressed Weld's face. "So you are." In a single, fluid motion, he clamped down on Weld's head and snapped the man's neck. The pitiful human slumped into Brasov's chair, dead.

This was why Brasov and vampire kind would win. Human beings were pitiful, weak creatures, who craved strong leadership. So weak were they that they would vote against their own self-interest, vote even to destroy themselves, if they thought some loftier, even impossible goal were being served. This suicidal notion was the very bedrock on which the Social Democrat party platform was built. Weld and his kind so fetishized anything more violent, more powerful than them, that they hastened to defend even the Sharia killings of their own kind. They put vampires like Brasov in power over them and then dared to believe they would not one day end up as cattle, as blood-slaves.

Brasov regretted the loss of Orin. It would be difficult to find another servant so willing... and so adept at Orin's tasks. He would probably have to replace Orin with two or more lesser operatives.

He took the transmitter handset from its cradle and keyed it. "This is Woodrow Brasov," he said. "Report, al Farir. Where is the Resistance now?"

"Sir?" came al Farir's voice. "I thought, when you did not respond—"

"I said *report*!"

"I am leading a column of Fedvamps to intercept Harden and the Resistance. We have received an alarm from the television station, WBSV, in Tampa. The rebels are attempting to take and hold it for some reason."

Brasov clenched the handset. "Not for *some* reason. The *only* reason. Harden has Adam. He is going to tell the world. He is going to broadcast Adam's identity, and mine, in hopes of undermining my authority. That must *not* be allowed to happen. Do whatever you must to establish that the Cousinry is responsible for murdering the world's oldest vampire. I don't care what measures you must take to ensure this."

"I will stop them, sir," said al Farir. "I will destroy them. I will kill Harden myself, and I will rip Adam's traitorous tongue from his mouth."

"See that you do."

"Yes, sir."

"And... Ibn al Farir?"

"Yes, sir?"

"If you fail me a second time, end your life. For I surely will when I find you."

"I understand, sir."

* * *

"Harden," said one of the Resistance soldiers through the radio, a man named Jeffreys. "We've got trouble. Basij militia are setting up outside. They've got federals with them. I'm looking at a cordon of MRAPs and wooden barricades with lots of guns behind them. There are Mutaween pickup trucks with mounted machineguns, too.

"We knew that was coming," said Harden into his own radio. "Keep an eye on them, Jeffreys. If they make a move, we'll have to redeploy to keep them out of the building long enough for us to finish the broadcast. Once we're done, we'll signal Remy for exfiltration again, and head to the roof for dust-off." There were rebels stationed at all entrances on the ground floor and at strategically placed windows. Their task was to repel any attempt to enter and retake the building. They would not be able to hold out forever, but they didn't need to. Once the broadcast was transmitted, they could go to ground.

"No," said Jeffreys. "That's what you don't understand, sir. One of the MRAPs is hauling what I think is an honest-to-God Rapier surface-to-air missile trailer. Remy's not going to be able to get anywhere near this place, not with that thing out there. They've set up MRAPs around it on all sides to screen it from our fire."

"That's not good," said Harden. The Rapier was a British-made SAM weapons system that had served the Brits well past 2020. Sales of weapons from England to Brasov's America had stepped up in the last two decades, Rapiers and upgraded Dagger Radar setups included. The missiles had very capable multi-beam high resolution 3D radar and target acquisition systems.

Around Harden, in the broadcast booth, Tag was directing the other rebels as they readied the main camera to transmit. Several of the station employees, including Alan Cord, were assisting. Harden had shown them his fangs and promised them he'd drink them all dry if they didn't do as they were told. He was lying through his considerable teeth, but they didn't know that.

Adam was propped up at the news desk, which had the most comfortable upholstered chair in the broadcast center.

"It gets worse," reported Jeffreys. "Harden, the Mutaween are hauling gasoline and carrying torches. They're getting ready to move on us under cover of a Fedvamp skirmish line. We can't get them all... and once they fire the building, it's only a matter of time before they burn us out or kill us."

"I understand." He paused, realizing what he was about to ask. "Jeffreys... I need you to hold as long as you can. There may be no escape for us. But if we can get this broadcast out... The rest of America may have a chance."

The radio was silent. Then Jeffrey's keyed his mic and said, "I understand, sir. We're all grateful to you."

"I wish I felt like I'd earned it," said Harden softly. "Out."

He clipped the radio back on his belt. Tag came to him and put her hand on his shoulder. "You did more than anyone else could."

"Getting us killed before this little revolution could begin wasn't my plan," he said, shooting her a lopsided grin.

"It's not a 'little revolution,'" she said. "And the Resistance has been raging for a long time. If this does what I think you believe it will... Well, things are going to change for Brasov. If we end up making the rest of his miserable eternal life a lot more difficult, I guess this mere mortal can die happy."

Harden looked deep into her eyes and pulled her close. He held her tightly, thinking about how little time they'd had, and how they might not have anymore. It seemed so unfair.

I'm sorry, Thomas, he thought. *I listened to what you were trying to tell me, finally. But I think I listened too late.*

"Mister Harden, sir?" said Cord meekly. "Everything's ready."

"What do I need to do to transmit?" asked Harden.

Cord indicated the camera, which was now trained on the anchor desk. "Just press this red button. As long as the light is on, the transmitter is hot and the signal is going out."

Harden reached behind himself, into the top of his pack, and pulled out his digital recorder. He removed the memory stick and showed it to Cord. "And this? I want to transmit the contents of this."

"Is that—?" Tag started to ask.

"It is," said Harden.

"This memory slot on the camera," said Cord. "It's set to autoplay. We use it for canned segments. Just enter the stick and it will roll as it loads."

"Good. Get out of here, Cord." He nodded to Tag, who radioed instructions to the Resistance fighters guarding the building. They would let the technicians leave the building unmolested.

"Sir?" said Cord. He clearly thought there was a bullet — or a vampire's fangs — in his future.

"You're free to go," Harden explained. "Get gone."

"Uh... Yes, sir! Thank you, sir!" The little man fled, followed by the other broadcast technicians.

"If they're lucky," said Tag, "the Fedvamps and Basij won't gun them down as they run from the building."

"Or execute them for helping us," said Harden. "I didn't want to put them in that position... but their job is pumping out propaganda for Brasov's police state. If they didn't understand the risks of that, well... I guess their allies among the Basij and the federals will explain it to them."

As much as he wanted to feel indifferent to it, it bothered Harden a great deal that the employees might die because of what he had to do. He was relieved when several minutes went by without reports of additional gunfire. He nodded to Tag again, motioning to his head as if holding an imaginary radio.

Tag nodded,. She keyed her mic again. "Jeffreys?" she said. "Status of the attack?"

"They're getting ready to move," Jeffreys replied. "I'd say your time is up."

Tag put her radio away. She entered the news room and put her hand on Adam's arm. The ancient vampire's eyes opened, slowly.

"Can you speak?" she asked him. "Do you have the strength?"

"Yes," said Adam. He straightened, abruptly vibrant. In a stronger voice than Harden would have thought possible, Adam said, "Should I start?"

Harden nodded. He pressed the red button on the camera.

"My name is Adam," said the world's oldest living vampire. "I am older than recorded time. I am a vampire, and for millennia, I have watched my fellow vampires. This broadcast is happening for one reason only. That is to tell you the truth about Woodrow Brasov."

The building began to shake. The federals were firing on them, perhaps even using RPGs or other explosives. They were softening up the Resistance defenses so the Basij could move in and fire the building.

"You have heard the rumors that Woodrow Brasov is secretly Vlad Tepes, the vampire known as Count Dracula. This is a lie. Dracula was one of our

155

kind, yes, and he did exist. He fought both as Vlad Tepes and under many identities after that, long after Vlad the Third was believed dead by humans. He was finally killed by Brasov, who assumed Dracula's identity. Brasov's ambitions were nothing less than world domination. Dracula's fame would help him accomplish that. The name of Vlad Tepes would give Brasov credibility among vampire kind that he might not otherwise have had."

Adam paused, faltering. Harden took an involuntary step forward, but the mysterious vampire managed to continue.

"Brasov was born Altan bin Ramseur, a Turk," said Adam. "I know because for thousands of years, I have made it my business to know what all of my fellow vampires were doing. Every one of you, every last vampire on the face of the Earth, is my descendant. I was the first. If you, listening to this, are vampire, your blood was mingled with mine. However indirectly, you are all my children."

Tag looked at Harden. Harden was not sure how to take that news. He shook his head.

"I have one message for you, all of you, whose undead lives are my doing, my fault, my responsibility. That message is that you *must* fight Brasov. You must turn against him, stand against him, and fight for your liberation. He does not care about vampires. He does not care about this nation. He does not care about making this world a better place. He cares only for power, for domination, and he will do whatever is necessary to take it by force. But there is more. You have not even begun to understand Brasov's murderous treachery. Whether you are vampire or human, whoever you are, if you value truth and freedom, you must know that Woodrow Brasov is a monster who must be stopped."

Here it comes, thought Harden.

"Woodrow Brasov's own agents committed the murders on what is known as the Day of the Rope, the slaughter of women and children, the killing of thousands of Muslims, in the newly established Sharia enclaves. For years the Cousinry has tried to tell you so. You did not believe them. But you must believe me, now. I tell you this as a fellow vampire. I tell you this as the oldest vampire. And to prove it to you, to show you that my words are truthful... and to show you that I am who I claim to be... I will do something that no other vampire could do. I will do something that I can do because, even after the torture I have suffered at Brasov's hands, I am stronger than any of my descendants. I don't know what makes me different. I only know that you must believe me. This is my final word to you, the vampire nation. The undead across America and throughout the world. This is my last will and testament. I am your father, Adam... and I am so sorry for what the world has become because of me."

A shrill alarm began to sound. Strobe lights set within the walls began to flash.

"This is Jeffreys!" shouted the Resistance fighter through their radios. "They've done it! They've set the building on fire!"

Adam stood. He reached up and grabbed his own head with both hands. As Harden, Tag, and others looked on in horror, he twisted his own skull free of his neck, ripping it off his body.

He did it without making another sound.

The head bounced across the desk and burst into flame. The body, too, spontaneously combusted. Both sublimated to ash in seconds, leaving nothing but a scorched residue behind.

Chapter Nineteen

Harden stared in disbelief. Blinking, he realized there was one more thing he had to do. He shoved the memory stick from his recorder into the television camera. In a few moments, the camera screen that had showed him Adam's shocking suicide was now playing Thomas Simpson's recorded message.

The building was shaking worse now. The barrage from outside was intensifying.

"We have to go!" shouted Tag.

Harden nodded. "You have heard my name," said Thomas Simpson on the screen behind him, "although you have not seen my face. In the year of our Lord 1066, at the Battle of Hastings, I was almost four months past my twentieth birthday. On that day I was turned. I became a vampire..."

They made their way down the stairs to the ground level and then to the lobby. The wreckage of the armored counter, the bodies of the dead, the damage done by the sustained fire from the cordon of federal troops and Fedvamps... all of this had turned the lobby into a charnel house. Harden took the lead, lowering his chin, walking to the edge of the lobby and the gaping holes now blown into the walls. Using the remains of the structure as cover, he shielded his eyes with one hand and looked out over the cordon. The smell of gasoline was thick. The Basij had apparently been lobbing unlit Molotovs at the face of the building, soaking it and the surrounding debris with fuel.

The fire would kill him just as certainly as it would kill Tag and the others. It would just take longer to do its job. A rifle round struck his chest. He staggered, but it wasn't bad. Tag ducked behind him instinctively. He had told her repeatedly to do so if the bullets started flying.

"Stubborn," she whispered.

"Stubborn," he said, nodding.

There were shouts from the cordon that Harden recognized as "cease fire." The incoming rounds stopped. A loudspeaker from somewhere along the cordon was being used to shout commands in Arabic. That would be the Basij leadership, readying their final assault.

Harden reached out and took Tag's hand without looking at her. She met his grip and squeezed.

"We got the transmission out," he said. "The world will know. The Resistance will go on.

"Yeah," said Tag. "I just wish..."

"Yeah," said Harden, nodding again. "Me too."

He closed his eyes and placed his arm around Tag. When the fire reached them, he would snap her neck. It would be quick and nearly painless. He would not allow her to burn to death.

"VINCENT HARDEN!" shouted an electrically amplified voice.

"Oh no," whispered Tag.

"VINCENT HARDEN!" shouted Ibn al Farir once more. "I will grant you a few more moments of life. I will do this for one reason. I wish you to face me so that I may tell President Brasov that I took your head personally."

"No," said Tag softly. "Don't do it. They'll kill us anyway."

"They will," said Harden. "But I can take him. The moment I do, they'll torch the building. Can you accept that?"

"I'd rather die here with you," she said. "Right now."

"If I remove Ibn al Farir, I damage Brasov," Harden said. "And I pay the federals back for Van Gogh."

Tag bit her lower lip. "All right," she finally said. "Here. Take this." She handed him her machete. "Kill him with something that was mine."

"I don't know if there's anything after we die," said Harden. "I used to believe in God. Now I don't know."

"I do," said Tag. "I'll believe for both of us."

"Then I'll see you," said Harden. "Tag... There's something I've wanted to tell you for a while." He shrugged out of his pack and dropped it at her feet. Then he leaned over and whispered into her ear.

"Tag's eyes widened, then narrowed. She looked at him and nodded."

"I love you too," she said.

Harden grinned. Then his expression changed. When he turned to face al Farir, there was nothing but murder written on his features.

The Basij were bickering with each other and trading words with al Farir. It was clear to Harden what was wrong. They weren't happy about delaying the plan to destroy the broadcast station just so al Farir could pursue a personal grudge. Al Farir, for his part, didn't give one solid damn what any of them thought about that.

He had told them to hold, though. That much was obvious. The flames that were going to destroy Harden and the Resistance would kill al Farir... although, as Harden closed with him, he realized that Ibn al Farir looked positively scorched. His skin was black and peeling across much of his body. His face looked distended. It wasn't healing properly, not with all that fire damage.

The hospital. He'd nearly bought it in the explosion.

Al Farir drew a curved sword from the scabbard on his back. It had a split blade, almost like a lizard's tongue. *Zulfiqar*, these were called. The word was floating around somewhere in Harden's overburdened memory. It was longer and heavier than Harden's substantial machete, but it would also be slower.

Al Farir took in Harden's blade and smiled. "Excellent," he said. "Excellent. So much better than before. Now face me, infidel. Face me and die in battle, knowing that your woman, your Resistance, your friends, your dreams die with you on this field."

Harden attacked.

He came at the vampire hard and fast, chopping and hacking with his machete. Al Farir countered blow for blow. He might be wounded, but he had lost nothing in speed and power. It occurred to Harden that in sheer age, he might well be much older, giving al Farir more power with which to work. As they fought, as their blades flashed and struck, as metal rang on metal, a sinking realization came over Vincent Harden.

He was not going to win.

Al Farir saw it too. The vampire began grinning like a crocodile, his strikes bolder, his steps more aggressive. He was dominating the space between them, wasting no time on idle words. His whole concentration was focused on a single goal: destroy Vincent Harden. Put the split tip of his Muslim sword in

Vincent Harden's heart. Remove Vincent Harden's head. Harden could not read his enemy's thoughts, but he could see it in al Farir's eyes. He could see the murder there, written more starkly than any urge for revenge, for justice, that Harden himself might feel.

Harden fought more recklessly. Ibn al Farir had to die. Even if every one of the Resistance present at the station died, their deaths would still have meaning. The video had gotten out; the Resistance would coalesce around a new leader. The secret of Brasov's treachery would erode support for the Brasov regime among the vampire nation. It was all worth it. It *had* to be. But if they could take out Brasov's most important lieutenant, they could hurt Brasov. And Harden wanted very much to hurt the man born as Altan bin Ramseur.

Ibn al Farir began toying with him. He would thrust with the blade, wait for Harden to sweep it aside, then step out again before stepping in at a new angle. He was the better swordsman; he was more experienced, more thoroughly trained. Harden had fought on many a battlefield, but he was hardly Miyamoto Musashi. He did not have Ibn al Farir's finesse. Harden was a ferocious hack-and-stab fighter. He had never mastered the finer points of dueling with a long blade.

Al Farir clearly had.

The enemy vampire slashed open Harden's left arm at the shoulder. He hacked again, more deeply, scoring another cut. Then he put all his weight behind the blade, hacking Harden's left arm again to the bone, driving the blade in with the back of hand on the sword's spine. Harden had time to register shock and surprise before al Farir withdrew the sword and raised it above his head.

"VINCENT!" shouted Tag.

He had time to turn and put out his hand as if to say, "No. Don't."

Al Farir chopped off Harden's bloody left arm.

The pain was unbelievable. Harden screamed, louder than he could re-member screaming. He had been wounded many times, but he had never lost a limb. Flashes, starbursts of light, appeared in his vision as the pain traveled through him in waves. He thought he could see his arm move; he thought he could feel the fingers of his left hand curling into a fist. He fell to his knees and dropped his machete. As if from miles away, his ears registered the clatter of the metal on the asphalt of the parking lot.

Harden. Harden. Harden. Why did he keep hearing his name?

Harden. Harden.

Was this shock? Was this what shock felt like?

"HARDEN!" Tag was screaming.

Ibn al Farir looked down on him, his scorched, mangled face split by a wide grin. "Her screams will be the last thing you hear," he said. "Perhaps I will put the Basij off a few minutes longer. Perhaps, in her final moments, she will be screaming *my* name."

There was more shouting from the cordon in Arabic. The Muslim militia were growing impatient.

Harden felt his blood roaring in his ears. He felt the fingers of his right hand flex. He felt the memory of his left hand. He stared down at the bloody stump where his left arm had been.

Ibn al Farir punched his fist into Harden's chest and ripped out Vincent Harden's beating heart.

Harden stared down at the hole in his body. He felt strangely numb. Al Farir was laughing. The sound was hollow, alien, in Harden's ears. He fought to stay conscious. He could not pass out. He had to live. He had to will his heart to grow back.

When he looked up again, he stared past al Farir, to the cordon. Something strange. What was *that*? That was the Rapier, the SAM unit that was preventing Remy from bringing in the chopper. But what was that heading toward it?

The streak of smoke moved in a straight line toward the SAM. When it struck, the Rapier trailer turned into a brilliant fireball. It was so bright, so hot, that Harden felt it on his face. The concussion struck him hard enough to make him sway on his knees. Even Ibn al Farir struggled to stay on his feet.

The sound of the explosion reached him.

The Cobra gunship swept over the line of Basij, its electric Gatling gun spraying the Muslim militia and the Fedvamps alike. The enemy were being blown apart. Another wave of attackers closed in from outside the cordon. They moved, and leapt, like vampires. They set upon the federals with reckless abandon, hacking with axes and swords, firing automatic weapons. By some miracle, the gasoline soaking the front of the broadcast station did not ignite. The fumes had faded; perhaps that immediate danger was gone.

But Harden wasn't thinking about that. He was looking at the woman who walked with her head high among the newcomers. She was incredibly beautiful. She carried a pair of Glock pistols.

And Vincent Harden had never hated anyone, even Brasov, as much as he hated her.

Elizabeth Hawkins met his gaze across the lot and through the carnage. She tossed him a mocking salute. Then she faded from view into the pall of black smoke from the Basij vehicles. The Cobra gunship's missiles had made short work of the column. The *whup-whup-whup* of the chopper grew more distant.

Ibn al Farir stood staring in disbelief.

Hawkins disappeared as quickly as she had arrived. Al Farir started; perhaps he had realized, only too abruptly, that he was now alone. The Basij and Fedvamps were dead, massacred in less time than it took to describe by Elizabeth Hawkins' blitzkrieg.

Why had she done it? Why had she helped him?

Ibn Al Farir began to laugh.

He started walking back to Harden, who knelt beside his own arm.

"HARDEN!" shouted Tag once more.

Ibn al Farir raised his sword. He did not speak. His face was a mask of fury.

Harden raised his right arm and let it fall.

"Now," he said, and fell backward onto the pavement.

Inside the broadcast building, sighting through the hole in the wall, Tag extended a LAWS rocket tube. It was the same one Harden had been carrying all this time inside the bedroll on his pack.

"When I tell you," he had whispered to Tag before the duel, "I want you to use it." She had told him she loved him.

Harden loved her, too.

The LAWS rocket had been a gift from Thomas Simpson. It seemed somehow fitting, now, that it be used to kill Brasov's most feared lieutenant.

The surprise Ibn al Farir must have felt had time to register on his face. Then the rocket struck him.

As Ibn al Farir disappeared in a ball of flaming gases and chunks of bloody meat, Tag ran for Harden. She threw her arms around him, holding him close, tears in her eyes.

"Come on," she said. "Come *on*! We've got to go. We've got to get clear before reinforcements come." The other surviving Resistance soldiers were with them now. Harden felt multiple sets of arms lift him up and carry him from the battlefield. He could hear a helicopter again, but the reverberation was different. He recognized the sound of Remy's Boeing. Someone had called in the chopper. There was no one left to stop them from escaping.

"Chopper," he said, his voice a croak. He tried to say more, but it didn't come out at first.

Tag leaned over him and whispered into his ear. "You're going to be okay," she said. "It's healing. I can see it healing. You're going to be okay."

"Stubborn," he whispered back.

Chapter Twenty

Tampa, Florida

Deputy Caliph Faisal opened his eyes. What had disturbed his sleep? He closed his eyes again, but it was no use; he suddenly felt wide awake. He got out of bed, shrugging into his robe and sandals. Perhaps a walk in the night air would help him to relax.

As he padded through the darkened temple, he knew a moment's regret. He wished the infidel whore were still in the recreation room. He would have to see to it that another Sharia violator were taken into custody as soon as possible. Someone young. Perhaps even younger than the last. He smiled at the thought of it.

God was great.

Considering his baser appetites, he realized he felt hungry. He went into the basement, where the kitchen and dining facilities were located. On the last step, he nearly fell. He had slipped in a puddle of liquid.

Had one of the kitchen staff spilled something? He would have them beaten for failing to clean it up. This was a holy place, both business center and mosque, where the work and the will of Allah was conducted. He reached out and touched the light switch on the wall. He would find the culprit and—

It was blood.

There was blood all over the floor. He could smell it, too; he did not know why he hadn't noticed it on entering. It was only when he reached the kitchen proper did he realize that Sampson was here, lying on his back. His dead eyes stared at the ceiling. His throat had been cut.

He heard movement behind him and whirled. There were five men standing there. They wore urban camouflage BDUs that were stained with blood at the arms and legs. In their hands were bloody knives, the heavy sort carried by combat troops.

"Who are you?" demanded Faisal. "How dare you enter this holy place? I am the Deputy Caliph of the Tampa enclave! You will pay for this desecration!"

One of the five stepped closer. He was smiling. When he opened his mouth, Faisal could see that he had *fangs*.

Vampires. These were not *men* at all. They were *vampires*.

"Everybody else is dead," said the creature. "There's just you, now."

"Who *are* you?" Faisal said again. "Why would one such as you... Why..."

"We're the New Resistance," said the creature, reaching out to grab Faisal by the throat. As he sunk his fangs deep into Faisal's neck, one of the other vampires spoke.

"You don't know us," he said. "But Brasov will, before we're done."

Deputy Caliph Faisal had no answer to that.

He was too busy trying to scream.

* * *

Outside Athens, Georgia

Harden sat up in bed. He tested his right arm experimentally, something he feared might become a bad habit. Tag kissed his bicep and spooned up next to him, pressing her naked body against his.

"You're doing it again," she whispered.

"I know," said Harden.

On finally returning to the bungalow, they had eaten and showered, then fallen almost immediately asleep. Once they both had a bit more energy, they had filled the late morning hours with... other things. It was the briefest of respites from the adventure they had just had and the many difficulties they would face.

"It's times like these," said Tag, resting her head on his chest, "that I think about becoming a smoking vampire."

"You're already smoking," said Harden.

Tag groaned. "You were never a comedian, were you?"

"No," said Harden, laughing. "I was a lot of other things."

"I want to hear about them," she said. "I want to hear everything about your life. Your *lifetimes*. You've seen so much, done so much. I want to know everything about you."

"We have time," said Harden.

"Do we?" she said. Sitting up again, she looked him in the eye. "Vincent, we're in very real danger. If we're not already on the federal Most Wanted lists, we soon will be."

"I know," said Harden. "To be honest, I don't think I'd want it any other way. It feels good to set aside all the pretending. To finally fight Brasov's evil directly. I'm not one for grand gestures, but if I could tell that bastard to his face that I'm coming for him, I would."

"Harden... You couldn't ever do that, could you? Rip your head off your own body to kill yourself?"

"No," said Harden. He almost laughed, or would have, had the subject not been so grim. "I've never seen a vampire do anything like that. I certainly don't know any who could, even after centuries. Vampires tend to grow stronger with age. Adam, as old as he was... There's no real telling what the limits of his strength might have been. Vampires don't burst into flame or turn to ashes. Adam is the only one I've ever seen do that. If he was born a vampire, while the rest of us were all turned, that might explain it. We may never know more than we do now. Not unless Adam left behind something for us to find."

"Like what?"

"A journal, maybe, like Thomas' diary. A recording. Hell, I'd settle for a set of vellum scrolls hidden in ancient pottery. Anything that could tell us more would be welcome. If there is something, and if Adam wanted us to find it, we will. If there isn't, or he didn't, that final speech is all we get."

"I've looked on the etherway. The video is there, and it's even made it to the outlawed Internet. There are some people saying it's fake, that it's all special effects. But there are a lot more people who seem to understand what it means. What it *could* mean."

"Thomas knew," said Harden. "He's says so in his journal. He was convinced that fighting Brasov with grassroots, with viral video, with underground newspapers and websites, with handheld *tracts* if that was what it took... he was sure that was the way. He believed in people in a way I didn't before. Maybe Adam once believed the same way."

"Do you think that's why he did it? Why he sacrificed himself that way? Or was it to get revenge on Brasov for torturing him?"

"No," said Harden. "I don't think so. He had the same look in his eyes that Thomas had at the end. I think he was simply... done. Done with living. Done with trying. So he gave us the greatest gift he could before the end. He knew what Brasov was, and that we have to fight him. So he gave us the best chance he could. He found one last fight worth giving his life to win. His gift is the foundation on which we'll build the Resistance now."

"Will it be enough?"

"It's going to have to be," said Harden. "I don't intend to live so long that I give up like Thomas. I don't want to escape this world like Adam. No matter how hard things get. I intend to fight until America is free again... or until I die fighting."

Tag fell against him, circling his chest with her arms. She hugged him tightly. "Let's not talk about that," she said. "Not right now."

"You're right," said Harden. He snuggled closer to her under the blanket, feeling her naked body against his. "Right now, we have much better things to do."

* * *

Through the thermal binoculars, Elizabeth Hawkins watched the two figures — one human, one vampire, from the heat patterns — press together for what must have been the sixth time in the last twelve hours. She frowned, feeling a pang of something, a feeling, that was alien to her. She chose not to deal with it, chose to tamp it down, chose to focus instead on what her next step must be.

Caspian crept up beside her. They watched the house from the cover of several similar structures across the street. Yards on this side of the street were narrow, creating dark alleyways in which they could hide.

"He is there?" asked Caspian.

"Yes," she said. "You did well, Caspian. Now we know where to lay hands on Harden if we must."

"You think we'll have to?"

"There's no way to tell," she said. "If nothing else, it's a very valuable piece of information. Vincent Harden is now not only the head of the Cousinry, but the leader of the Resistance. *Everybody* is going to want a piece of him." She lowered the binoculars. "Bring the car around back. We need to get to Tennessee to meet with the Apostates for Liberty. If I promise to turn a few of them, we might be able to get the whole cell to come over to our side."

Caspian snorted. "They are anarchists," he said. "Terrorists. Even the Resistance is not sure what to do with them."

"Which is why they might well be perfect for us," she said. "Go now. We have much work to do."

Caspian nodded and disappeared into the night.

Brasov's power was in jeopardy. Already, among the vampire nation, there were rumblings among his former loyalists that perhaps the Cousinry... or Elizabeth Hawkins... represented the better path. She would have many hard weeks ahead of her if she hoped to siphon off more support for her cause. And she would have to walk a fine line, maintaining her alliance with the Cousinry while also looking out for her own interests.

The feeling she could not name stabbed her again as she looked once more into the binoculars. Damn Vincent Harden anyway. Who was he to her? Why should she care if he chose to bed some human whore, some Resistance camp trollop?

But she did.

She cared very much.

As she spied on Harden and his human lover, her hands gripped the binoculars tightly enough to crimp the aluminum.

* * *

Washington, District of Brasovia

Woodrow Brasov sat at the Resolute Desk, staring at the glass wedge of the etherway tablet propped on the desktop. His jaw was very tight. The anger smoldering in his eyes was enough to torch a village. It was enough for a hundred villages. It was the anger of a man who sees his carefully laid plans threatened by forces he has not anticipated.

"...Before I die, however, I wish to say one more thing," said a dying Thomas Simpson to the camera. The video clip sharing site indicated this particular recording had been copied and shared fully *eight million* times. The count was still climbing.

"The Cousinry is not the enemy of society," Simpson went on. "Woodrow Brasov is. He must be stopped. His plan is to rule completely, unquestioned and unquestionable, over a divided, dispirited world. But you can fight him."

Brasov stood. He turned to gaze out the explosive-proof, floor-to-ceiling "glass" windows behind his desk.

"Take up arms," said the recording of Simpson. "Stand your ground. Refuse to comply. Brasov is a vampire, yes. Worse, he is a monster. But he is not invulnerable. He is not invincible. Fight him. Fight his forces. Die on your feet. Or live forever on your knees under the yoke... of his... oppression..."

Brasov clasped his arms behind his back and stared at nothing. His mind was filled with thoughts of the challenges that lay ahead.

He stood there for a long time.

Coming Soon!

Jerry and Sharon Ahern's
AMERICA UNDEAD
America Burning
Book 2
by
Phil Elmore

The revolution against the tyrannical undead government of vampire President For Life Woodrow Brasov has only just begun. As a new Resistance to Brasov's suppressive regime grows in strength, the Cousinry and its allies—human and vampire—are poised to make real gains in their fight for liberty. But Brasov is not about to release his iron grip on power... and he has a terrible weapon at his disposal that just might break the Resistance forever.

For more information
visit: www.speakingvolumes.us

On Sale Now!

DON'T BE A STATISTIC, BE A SURVIVOR!

SURVIVE!
by
Jerry Ahern

For more information
visit: www.speakingvolumes.us

COMING SOON!

SURVIVE!
LIVE WELL AND LIVE WISELY
Volume 1

**MONEY SHOULD NOT DETERMINE HOW WELL YOU LIVE.
SURVIVE, SUCCEED AND ACHIEVE SUCCESS.**

**For more information
visit:** www.speakingvolumes.us

FOR MORE EXCITING BOOKS, E-BOOKS, AUDIOBOOKS AND MORE

visit us at
www.speakingvolumes.us

Sign up for free and bargain books

Join the Speaking Volumes mailing list

Text

ILOVEBOOKS

to 22828 to get started.

Message and data rates may apply.

www.ingramcontent.com/pod-product-compliance
Lightning Source LLC
Chambersburg PA
CBHW020612250626
47154CB00004B/1476